COMPLETELY CHLOE

Also in the Strawberry Sisters series:

Perfectly Ella
Especially Amelia

Older books by Candy Harper:

Have a Little Faith
Keep the Faith
Leap of Faith

COMPLETELY CHLOE

CANDY HARPER

SIMON & SCHUSTER

First published in Great Britain in 2017 by Simon & Schuster UK Ltd
A CBS COMPANY

Copyright © 2017 Candy Harper

1 3 5 7 9 10 8 6 4 2

Simon & Schuster UK Ltd
1st Floor, 222 Gray's Inn Road
London WC1X 8HB

www.simonandschuster.co.uk

Simon & Schuster Australia, Sydney
Simon & Schuster India, New Delhi

A CIP catalogue record for this book
is available from the British Library.

PB ISBN 978-1-4711-4710-4
eBook ISBN 978-1-4711-4711-1

This book is a work of fiction. Names, characters, places and
incidents are either the product of the author's imagination or are
used fictitiously. Any resemblance to actual people living or
dead, events or locales is entirely coincidental.

Typeset in Bembo by M Rules
Printed and bound by CPI Group (UK) Ltd, Croydon, CR0 4YY

Simon & Schuster UK Ltd are committed to sourcing paper
that is made from wood grown in sustainable forests and support the Forest
Stewardship Council, the leading international forest certification organisation.
Our books displaying the FSC logo are printed on FSC certified paper.

For Io, Isla, Carys and Gabrielle

CHAPTER ❤ ONE

People are always looking for things in my house.
Things that have mysteriously disappeared. Clean
pants. A hairbrush. Their homework. The last
chocolate biscuit (good luck finding that because
I've usually eaten it). Sometimes stuff turns up;
usually when Mum says the house looks like a pack
of trolls have moved in and she threatens to throw
everything in the bin, then we have a big tidy and
we find whatever we're looking for in the rabbit
hutch or under the bath mat. But sometimes our
things seem to have actually melted away.

My dad's house is not like that at all. My dad
and his girlfriend, Suvi, tell us that their house is
our home too, and it sort of is, because me and my
three sisters go there every Wednesday and every
other weekend, but it looks very different. There

1

are whole walls in their house that have nothing on them: no photos, no posters, and, even though they have got a seven-month-old baby, no sticky handprints.

In their hallway, there is a shelf that has just one vase on. An empty vase. All their books are organised in height order, like kids in a school photo. You have to put shoes away in a special cupboard just for shoes. You put them on a rack and close the door as if you weren't going to have to get them right back out again in a little while anyway.

If you put anything down at my dad's house it gets picked up and put in a little basket or hidden in a drawer.

On Saturdays, at home, when it's time for my rugby training session, I normally do this mad run round the house to find all my stuff. My boots always seem to be in two different rooms, which is funny because I never remember hopping about with just one boot on. Then my kit is usually hanging on the clothes airer or sometimes it's still in my bag from the week before.

Of course, at Dad's house, it's the complete opposite.

On the last Saturday of the Easter holidays my dad came downstairs with hair wet from the shower and said, 'Is your rugby stuff ready?'

Normally when I go to Dad's I have to hang my rugby things on a special peg in the hall, but this week I hadn't brought them with me.

'I don't need them today,' I said.

'Oh? Has training been cancelled? I didn't get an email.'

'I'm going to a paintball party. Thunder's mum is picking me up.'

Dad combed his wet hair with his fingers. 'And that's okay with your coach, is it?'

'It's fine. People miss sessions all the time.'

'Seems a bit slack to miss rugby just because you've had a better offer.'

I stared at Dad. 'But that's exactly *why* I'm doing paintballing instead of rugby. Because it's more fun.'

Dad's forehead creased up. 'But you made a commitment to rugby.'

'I'll be committed next week. It's only one session.'

He hesitated and I knew he wasn't sure. 'Mum knows,' I said. I was pretty certain that would seal the deal because my dad doesn't really like making the kind of decisions where he has to get tough.

'Well,' he said. 'I suppose that's all right then.'

I nodded and went into the kitchen to get started on breakfast. When you're going to spend the morning running about shooting people, I find it's good to get three or four courses inside you.

My sister Amelia was sitting at the table. Even though she's fourteen and I'm twelve, she's much smaller and skinnier than me so it wasn't very hard to budge her up along the bench by pushing her with my hip.

'Hey!' she said, trying to swat me away. 'You could just ask politely.'

'Would you have moved if I'd asked politely?'

'No.'

'That's why I have to use muscle power.'

'Butt power, more like.'

I leant across the table and grabbed a box of cereal.

'Speaking of butts,' she said, 'I saw how much chilli you ate last night so keep that thing pointed away from me.'

I gave her my most menacing grin. 'Don't worry, if I feel any rumblings I'll make sure I sit on you.'

Amelia rolled her eyes. 'Don't you have to get off to rugby?' she asked.

'Nah, giving it a miss this week.'

'Again? I thought you liked rugby.'

'I do. It's brilliant.' I crushed my cornflakes down with my spoon so that I could fit more in the bowl. 'The problem is that what I like best is just

4

doing it. When we go to practice, we have to do all this stretching and running laps and when we finally get the ball they make us do the same pass over and over again.'

'Isn't that all the stuff you have to do to get good?'

'I s'pose.' I stuck out my bottom lip and blew up at my fringe. 'And I have been doing it all. It's just that Coach thinks we should do it in silence or something. He gets snotty just because I tell a joke or do an impression.'

'That does seem a bit uptight.'

'He says I'm distracting everyone.'

Amelia squinted at me. 'And are you? Because I still get distracted thinking about that time you did the warthog impression, even now. In fact, it's probably going to affect my GCSE results.'

Amelia laughed so hard at my warthog impression that she popped her trouser button undone, but now she pretends she was traumatised by it.

'It's not my fault if I'm extremely funny,' I said. 'I can't help it if I make people at rugby roll about laughing and then maybe one of them clutches at the drinks table and all the drinks go on the floor.'

Amelia moved her glass of orange juice further away from me. 'Hmm. So maybe it's not that your coach wants you to be completely silent and more that he wants you to stop causing total chaos. That sounds reasonable.'

Amelia finished her breakfast and cleared away her plate. I started on my toast course and wondered if it was true that Coach wanted me to stop 'causing chaos'. It was easy for Amelia to say that seemed reasonable, but it really wasn't, because I honestly can't help the way that people laugh so hard around me. Sometimes I'm not even trying to be funny. Sometimes I'm just eating a really large sandwich in a hurry.

I polished off my toast plus two boiled eggs and a cereal bar while thinking about Coach, then I totally forgot all about rugby practice as soon as I got in the car with Thunder. There wasn't an awful lot of room for me next to him on the backseat because Thunder is nearly six foot tall and about the same distance around the middle. Some of the Year Sevens are scared of Thunder, but he's my best mate and I know he's just a big softie who loves puppies and the Cookie Monster. He also loves rugby, and wrestling and pickle and crisp sandwiches, which is good because those are some of my favourite things. We hang out and do loads of cool stuff, but this was our first time paintballing together. I absolutely love paintballing. I like the

6

running and the hiding and being on a team and getting messy and shooting people. I especially love shooting people. The one thing I don't like is the safety lecture.

Once we'd arrived and handed in the form that your parents have to sign to say you won't sue them if someone blinds you with paint, they kitted us out with a helmet and the guns and ammo, and then we had to sit and listen to their boring safety lecture even though I told them that I'd already heard it. While they were dribbling on, I thought out my plan of attack.

'Okay, guys!' the man in charge said and I realised we were finally about to start. 'Keep it safe and have fun!'

We were in two teams. Because it was Shania's birthday party she was captain of our team. 'You two head over that way,' she said to me and Thunder.

We scooted off into the trees in the direction she pointed but once we were out of sight I pulled Thunder in the opposite direction.

'But Shania . . .' he started.

'Listen,' I said. 'I've been here before and I know the best spot for maximum casualties.' I led him to a place in the woods where the trees thinned out. 'Now, we stay hidden in the trees but every time some idiot makes a break across the clearing . . .' I lifted my gun and mimed a shot. 'We pick them off.'

'Nice,' Thunder laughed. 'Where shall we hide?'

In the end we managed to squeeze practically underneath a bush. You wouldn't even have known we were there until you got really close, but no one did get close because we had a clear view of anyone approaching and we took them straight down.

It was fun to start with, but after we'd taken out half of the opposite team I started to get restless. I looked at my watch and I knew that our session would soon be over.

'This is too easy,' I said to Thunder. 'How about we try to make it back to base?'

'Are you kidding? We've managed to get this far without a drop of paint on us. If we break cover someone will shoot us.'

'Yeah, but it's more of a challenge when we're out in the open, isn't it? Come on, let's do it!' I wriggled out of the bush and started creeping back towards the base building where we started.

Thunder was muttering under his breath, but he followed me anyway. We got all the way round the edge of the clearing, then I spotted someone crouched low on our left.

'Take cover,' I hissed to Thunder. We threw

ourselves behind a tree while whoever it was fired off shot after shot in a pretty stupid way because then they had to reload and we sped off. The long, low base was in sight now but I could hear that there were people in the greenery around us. We slowed to a standstill.

Thunder was a few paces in front of me.

'Shall we make a run for it?' he asked.

'No, keep down and cree—' That's when I saw a flash of reflected light. The sun was bouncing off someone's goggles. Someone dead ahead in the bushes. Even as I clocked the boy he was raising his gun to point directly at Thunder. 'Nooooo!' I sprang forwards, knocking Thunder off his feet so we both crashed down on the grass.

I scrambled into a sitting position and let off two quick shots, hitting the boy on the shoulder.

The final whistle blew.

I looked at Thunder and raised my hand for a high five.

'Not a drop!' he said.

We trooped back inside base and checked out everyone else. We were the only ones to get away without being hit.

'What happened to you?' I asked Shania. 'Did you get your gun the wrong way round and shoot yourself?'

She was absolutely plastered with paint splats.

'What happened to me?' she snapped. 'What happened to you? I came through your section and shouted at you to cover me. You didn't make a single shot. Where were you?'

I felt a bit bad. A good soldier should look after his comrades, but Thunder and I were pretty busy taking down the enemy and that's the main thing, isn't it? 'Soz, Shania! I didn't mean to leave you without back up.'

She was still scowling.

I don't know why she wasn't letting it go. I'd be pleased my teammates had done so well. 'Look on the bright side; Thunder and I did some serious damage to the other team. We've definitely won.'

She grunted, though I'm pretty sure it cheered her up when our team were declared the winners. Winning is the best.

When Thunder's mum dropped me back at Dad's, I was still buzzing.

'Did you have a good time?' Dad asked.

'It was brilliant! We slaughtered them!'

'Well done. You certainly look like you threw yourself into it.'

'She looks like she threw herself into a swamp,' Amelia said, eyeing my muddy face.

'You can't win a war and keep your nails nice,' I said.

Dad stepped between us. 'Go and get your face clean because we're going to McDonald's for a late lunch.'

'Yes!' I did a fist pump. I scooted up the stairs to get clean. This day was turning out pretty well. All I needed was an action film on TV tonight and an extra-large chocolate cheesecake and it would be perfect.

Even though my dad bought a big seven-seater last year so that he, Suvi, me, Amelia and my two youngest sisters, Ella and Lucy, plus the baby can all travel together in one car, Suvi said she'd rather stay at home with baby Kirsti and have a sandwich.

'We could bring you back a cheeseburger,' I said.

'I prefer my sandwich,' Suvi said.

'Chicken Royale?' I suggested.

'No.'

'Filet-O-Fish? Big Mac? McFlurry?'

'Thank you, Chloe, but I don't want any of these things.'

Suvi is a bit weird sometimes. She thinks sugar is evil and she gets excited about cooking stuff for tea called things like *Rainbow Salad* and *Chargrilled Super Vegetables*. 'Really? There's absolutely nothing at McDonald's that you'd like to eat?'

She smiled and shook her head.

I could hardly believe it. I like Suvi, but I will never understand her.

When we got to McDonald's, I sat next to Ella. Ella is a year younger than me. She likes books and maths and being kind. She also doesn't mind if you help her finish her fries.

'Will you get into trouble for missing rugby?' she asked me.

I hadn't thought about rugby all morning. I wasn't really worried about it. I can't see the point of worrying about trouble before the trouble happens.

'Coach will probably just think I was ill,' I said.

Ella sipped her drink. 'But that's lying.'

I chewed on my burger and thought about it. I don't really like telling lies. Mum has made me learn some of those polite lies, you know, like *'Mm, this is delicious.'* And *'Oh, wow, Granny, I've always wanted one of these.'* I still think they're pretty stupid because how is anyone ever going to get any better at cooking if people don't tell them that their stew is disgusting and how could Granny possibly believe that anyone would want a sewing basket? But I say them anyway because Mum says you have to so that people's feelings don't get hurt. I don't lie about things that I've done, though, because I don't think that's right. Sometimes I do dumb stuff and that gets me into trouble but I don't lie because that would be cowardly. If you do something you have to take the telling off that comes with it.

'I didn't say that I would actually tell him I was ill. If he asks me where I was then I'll tell him I was paintballing.'

Ella's forehead crumpled and I could tell that she was worrying about it for me.

'It'll be fine,' I said, offering her some of Amelia's chicken nuggets.

When we were done, we came out into the car park and I said, 'Watch this, Lucy.'

Lucy used to be the youngest before baby Kirsti came along. She's seven years old and has shiny red-gold curls that make her look like a little angel. She's not a little angel. But she is the kind of person who is impressed by leapfrogging over bins, so I took a run up, gave a whoop and leapfrogged over three in a row. I'm pretty good at leapfrogging. Lucy and Ella clapped and some teenagers getting out of a car whistled. I took a bow and as I stood up, Lucy pointed across the car park. 'Isn't that your coach?'

I looked over. There was my rugby coach. Standing next to his car, staring right at me.

I sort of froze.

Lucy waved.

13

'Stop it!' I said. 'He's going to wonder what I'm doing here when I didn't go to training.'

'Oh,' said Lucy, still waving. 'I bet you wish you didn't do such a loud whoop now.'

Even though I thought there was no reason why I shouldn't go to McDonald's if I wanted to, I sort of did wish it.

'Because if you hadn't done that he probably wouldn't have noticed you, would he?'

'Shhh,' I said. I thought Coach would come over and ask me why I'd missed practice because he definitely saw me, but he just stared for a little bit longer and then got into his car and drove off. I had a sort of squirmy feeling inside but that was probably just the extra-large Fanta I'd had sloshing about.

'Are you worried about getting told off?' Lucy asked.

'No,' I said, trying to squash the squirminess down. 'It's just one session. Well, maybe a few sessions this year. It's not like I've done a crime or anything.' Which was true, but something about the look on Coach's face meant that I wasn't exactly looking forward to hearing what he had to say to me.

CHAPTER ❤ TWO

It's always a bit of shock when the holidays finish and you have to go back to school. I managed to survive the first Monday back even though I got two lots of homework from teachers who didn't seem to care that I needed time to get used to having to use my brain again. I decided to do both pieces of work as soon as I got in so that I could enjoy the rest of my evening.

I'd just got myself comfortable on the sofa with two packets of crisps, three cushions and an episode of *The Simpsons* when I looked up and saw my little sister Lucy standing in the doorway with her face all scrunched up and angry.

'Why are you looking like that?' I asked.

She flopped down in an armchair. 'Like what?'

I opened my packet of cheese and onion crisps

and mixed them together with the spicy chilli ones. 'Grumpy. I mean, you always look like the angry little one from *The Moomins* who likes shouting and stamping her feet, but your face is especially twisted up today. You look like you're chewing on a wasp.'

'It was the old lady,' Lucy said, as if that was a perfectly good explanation.

'What old lady?'

'The one next door.'

Our next-door neighbour is a very boring man who never does anything interesting, but recently his mum has come to stay with him. She's a little bit interesting because I have never seen anyone so wrinkly before.

'What about her?' I asked through a mouthful of crisps.

'She threw a marrow at me.'

Which did sound harsh, but I've thrown quite a lot of stuff at Lucy myself and I can tell you that she always started it. 'What did you do?'

Lucy scrunched her face even tighter. 'I didn't do anything! I was just being me in the garden and then she threw a marrow at me!'

If you know Lucy then you know that whenever she says 'I was just ...' it means she was doing something incredibly annoying.

'How exactly were you being you?' I asked.

'Just being happy and cheerful like I normally am.'

'You are not cheerful.' I had a thought. 'Were you singing?'

'I can sing in my garden if I want to!'

Lucy only sings one song. It's about a duck who keeps trying to buy grapes from a lemonade stand and the lemonade-stand man keeps telling him that he only sells lemonade and he hasn't got any grapes and the duck keeps asking and asking. He's a very stupid duck. If I was the lemonade-stand man, that song would end up with me having crispy-duck pancakes.

'Was it the duck song?' I asked.

'What if it was the duck song? I was just singing for hardly even an hour and then she throws a marrow at me.'

'An hour? I'm amazed that she didn't throw a spade at you.'

'She tried to. She wasn't strong enough to get it over the fence.'

'Girls! Tea time!' Mum called from the kitchen.

I crammed the last of my crisps into my mouth and we went and sat down at the table.

Lucy forgot about the old lady because Amelia was moaning and pouting and flicking her hair about so it ended up in other people's cottage pie.

'Are you all right?' Ella asked her. Which was a big mistake, because when you ask Amelia what the matter is she always tells you, and she doesn't give you the short version either.

'Lauren's mum says she can't do school choir this term because she gets too tired in the late afternoon,' Amelia whined. 'It was bad enough when she missed the Christmas concert, but now she won't be in the summer celebration and—'

'I thought she was better,' I said, so that we could get to the point.

Amelia looked down her nose at me. 'You don't just get better from Chronic Fatigue Syndrome.' Then she softened a bit. 'Actually, she has been coping better recently but her mum says that's because they've worked out what she can manage and that she has to know her limits. That means no after-school clubs or going out in the evening, so no choir.'

'That's not much fun for Lauren,' Mum said. 'Is she going to cut down her school days?'

Amelia shook her head. 'Not if they can help it. She's already on mornings only; her mum says school has to come before extra-curricular activities.'

'Maybe you should think about cutting down my school days, Mum,' I said with my best puppy-dog eyes.

Lucy laughed.

Mum shook her head.

'It's not really funny,' Amelia said. 'School is pretty lame but imagine being too weak to even walk there.'

I couldn't imagine that. I couldn't imagine not being able to run and jump and rugby tackle. 'Poor Lauren,' I said.

'Yes,' Mum said putting an arm around Amelia. 'It's tough.'

Amelia took that as encouragement to start sighing again. 'I miss singing with her,' she said. 'I was looking forward to rehearsing for the summer celebration but it won't be the same. Part of the fun of doing shows is doing it with Lauren.'

'Can't you do singing somewhere else?' I asked.

'Yes!' Ella said. 'You could join one of those community choirs!'

Amelia didn't look very enthusiastic. 'It doesn't matter where it is – she can't do anything in the evening. Or anything after four o'clock really.'

'Then find something in the morning, dummy,' Lucy said.

Amelia curled her lip. You'd have thought that we were trying to get her to eat slugs. 'Where am I going to find somewhere like that?' she asked.

'Online?' Ella suggested in a tiny voice.

Amelia looked at Ella. 'I suppose if it was at the weekend and not too late then Lauren's mum might agree.'

Mum nodded encouragingly. 'Why don't you try having a look to see if you can find something local?'

'Okay, I'll look,' Amelia said, as if she was doing us a favour.

I wasn't completely convinced that she thought it was a good idea or that she'd bother going online, but I could see that she was trying really hard not to be sarky with Ella. So I thought it was best to move things on. 'Mum,' I said with my best winning-smile. 'How much of a jar of peanut butter would you say it was reasonable to put into a smoothie?'

Mum folded her arms and reminded me she'd only just bought that jar of peanut butter, but she still let me make everyone choco–nut smoothies for pudding.

CHAPTER ✦ THREE

At lunch the next day, my friend Amirah, who goes to rugby and is in my PE class, came up to me and asked where I was on Saturday. I told her I was paintballing.

'Uh-oh,' she said. 'Coach won't like that. He got really ratty with me just because I missed a couple of sessions to go shopping.'

I knew she was right but there was no point in getting upset about it, and anyway, I needed all of my energy because it was time for chemistry, and Mr Chadwick is the kind of teacher who thinks that you should always be on time to his lesson and on top of that he doesn't just want your body in the classroom; he expects your whole mind too.

Some teachers will let you get away with staring

into space and never answering any questions, as long as you're quiet and get some of the work written in your book. Mr Chadwick is not like that. He expects you to totally concentrate on science and if he thinks you're drifting off to think about something more interesting, like what's for lunch or who would win a zombies vs. vampires battle, then he pounces on you and says, 'Perhaps Chloe would like to explain this to everyone,' when he knows that you would not like it, you would not like it at all because you've got no idea what he was dribbling on about.

I've worked out a system to beat him at his own game, though. As soon as he starts explaining something I put my ears on high alert and listen to everything he says and make little notes in my book so that I always know the answers to his questions. You'd think that he'd be happy that I'm listening to his blabbering, but he still finds something to moan about. If he can't complain about me not paying attention then he tells me to stop slouching or that my shirt is hanging out. I don't care much but it makes me mad when he starts saying the same sort of thing about Thunder because even though Thunder looks tough he gets flustered really easily. When Mr Chadwick starts picking holes in him he can't get his words out properly and he turns bright pink. It's really unfair to make fun of someone like that.

So usually in chemistry I have to concentrate hard to make sure I know what we're learning and to keep Thunder up to speed. Paying attention is really tiring, though, and by home time I was worn out. I only had room in my mind for embarrassing accidents that might happen to Mr Chadwick and I totally wasn't thinking about what Amirah had said about Coach.

I met Amelia and Ella at the gates so we could walk home together and I told them exactly what I thought of Mr Chadwick and how having to concentrate for every minute of his lessons is exhausting me.

'What about you, Ella?' I asked, when I'd finished moaning. 'How was your day?'

'It was okay.'

I turned to look at her. Normally, Ella thinks school is 'brilliant' and 'really fun'. Something horrible must have happened.

'Has someone been mean to you?' Amelia asked.

Ella's face was turning pink. 'No, it isn't anything like that. It's a good thing really.'

'You're not wearing a good-thing face,' I said.

Ella took a deep breath. 'I'm going to be on the Student Council.'

Amelia whistled. 'Wow. How come? I thought they chose people for that ages ago.'

'They did, but our class chose Ibrahim and now he's left to go to another school.'

'So your class voted for you instead?' I asked.

Ella looked guilty. 'No. Miss Espinoza just remembered that there was a meeting today as we were going out of registration, so she said I'd better go because I'm tutor captain.'

'She probably asked you because she thought you'd do a good job,' Amelia said.

I nodded. 'And our tutor is always telling us what a brilliant way it is to get involved with running the school. I bet I could get people to vote for me, but I've never decided to do it because you have to do stuff in lunchtime and I don't want to do that because I need my lunchtimes for lunch. And maybe some football, but mostly lunch.'

Ella's eyes were big and sad, like a kitten's on a Christmas card. I didn't understand what the problem was.

'It's nothing to worry about,' I said. 'What was the meeting like? Did you talk to the head boy?'

Ella looked horrified. 'Of course I didn't. Actually, I didn't talk to anyone at all.'

'Why not?'

'I couldn't think of anything clever to say. And

even if I could have, I don't think I would have been able to say it in front of all those people.'

'You go to tutor captains' meetings,' Amelia pointed out.

'That's only for Key Stage 3. No one there is any older than you. At Student Council some of them are basically grown-ups.'

Amelia pulled a face. 'They're just people.'

'They're all super confident and have brilliant ideas and can explain them without getting their words all twisted up.'

I put an arm around Ella. I wish she could know how brilliant she is; if she did, then she'd be super confident too. 'If you don't like it, why don't you tell Miss Espinoza that you don't want to do it?'

Ella shook her head. 'I don't think I should just give up.'

'You'll probably feel braver at the next meeting,' Amelia said.

We all knew that wasn't very likely, but it was like those lies that Mum taught me; it was meant to help Ella, so I said, 'Of course you will.'

CHAPTER ✦ FOUR

'Lucy, you did clean your teeth, didn't you?' Ella asked.

It was Wednesday and Dad had picked us up from school to take us straight to the dentist. Lucy was already in the car, strapped into her booster seat and wearing one of Kirsti's old baby vests as a hat.

Lucy folded her arms across her chest. 'Dad's already asked me that!'

'You haven't actually answered the question,' I said.

'Yes! I've cleaned my teeth. Why does everybody keep asking?'

'Oh, I don't know,' Amelia said turning up the sarcasm. 'Maybe it's because last time we went to the dentist you hadn't done it and then we all got to be super embarrassed when the dentist found brown and green bits between your teeth.'

'I thought it would be more interesting for him. It must be really boring looking at shiny clean teeth all day.'

'Yeah,' Amelia said. 'But the answer to that is to get a job that's better than being a dentist, not to try looking at skanky teeth instead.'

Lucy looked offended. 'My teeth weren't skanky. They were just . . . colourful.'

Amelia snorted.

'I have checked Lucy's teeth,' Dad interrupted. 'And they are ready for inspection. How about you, girls? Did you manage to do yours?'

I flashed him my toothiest smile. 'Yep. But we did have to wait ages for Ella.'

Ella wriggled. She doesn't like to be late. 'I had to wait till the loos were empty. I didn't want anyone to think I was weird because I was cleaning my teeth at school.'

Lucy leant forward to look at Ella. 'I don't know why you don't like people thinking you're weird. I'd love it for people to think I'm weird.'

Amelia reached back from the front passenger seat and pulled Lucy's vest-hat down over her eyes. 'Don't worry, titch, they already do.'

I know some people are scared of going to the

dentist, but I like it. I love the medicine smell and I like the chair. When I was little, I used to pretend I was an astronaut and I was sitting in a rocket seat getting ready to blast off.

The dentist checked my teeth and told her assistant what to put on my record on the computer. Then I sat up and said, 'Can I ask you something?'

'Of course.' She smiled.

Amelia didn't smile. She frowned. She thinks I talk too much and that I'm always wasting people's time but if people didn't want to talk to me they would just say so, wouldn't they? And anyway, I am pretty interesting.

'I've got a rugby training camp coming up,' I said. 'And I was wondering what the best kind of gum shield is?'

'Ah, that's a good question.'

I gave Amelia a look but she was pretending to fall asleep.

'The very best are the kind where they take a mould of your teeth and make a shield that is perfectly fitted to your mouth. If you wanted one of those, I have a leaflet about them but they can be pretty pricey. If you want something cheaper, then the kind you get in sports stores are fine as long as you remould them regularly to make sure it fits. Your teeth are still moving around in your mouth.'

She paused to change the cup of pink stuff that you rinse with. 'The most important thing of all is that you remember to wear it. Sports can be bad news for teeth if you don't protect them.'

'Thank you,' I said. 'I'll remember all that.' I took one of the leaflets she offered me, even though I didn't think Mum would want to pay for a gum shield that cost more than my rugby kit. I thought maybe she would let me get a new one of my usual brand, though. I fancied a neon-green one this time.

I wanted to make sure I was totally prepared for camp. Coach had been telling us about it all last term. Our local rugby club has been running an intensive training camp for boys for years, but this was only the second time that they were doing a girls' camp too. Coaches all over the South West were allowed to pick their very best players to attend. Everybody knows that, along with Amirah, I'm the best player on our squad and I couldn't wait to get to camp and spend a whole week playing rugby all day long. Last year they even had special sessions with actual rugby players from proper teams. Imagine how brilliant that would be!

On the way home, Dad told us how pleased he was with us all for taking good care of our teeth.

Amelia pulled a face but I know she likes it when Dad says nice stuff to her.

'And well done, you,' he said to me. 'I didn't know that Coach had announced who had been chosen for the training camp.'

'He hasn't,' I said. 'Not officially anyway.'

'How do you know you're going, then?' Ella asked. 'How many people get chosen?'

'Three,' I said, rubbing my teeth so they squeaked.

'Three! Out of all the girls who train?' She looked worried.

I nodded.

'Well, Chloe,' Dad said. 'That's not very many, so don't be disappointed if you don't get picked.'

I laughed. 'I'm not going to be disappointed.'

'Look!' Lucy said, pointing out the window. 'It's Ella's favourite place: the Ghost School.'

We all turned to look, except Ella, who stayed staring in the opposite direction. 'Don't, Lucy,' she said.

We were driving past Westbrook Primary School. It's been closed down for years and it always creeps Ella out because people tell spooky stories about it.

Lucy grabbed Ella's arm. 'I can see a face! I can see that ghost girl who curses people!'

Ella pushed Lucy's hand off.

'You're such an idiot,' I said to Lucy.

'Girls,' Dad said in his warning voice.

'I did see someone!' Lucy insisted. 'And she was all like this . . .' She stretched her face into a silent scream.

Ella shivered.

'There wasn't anyone there,' I told her.

'There was!' Lucy said. 'You just can't see her because you're too, too . . . boring and you only think about rugby and not anything interesting like ghosts. All you care about is stupid rugby.'

'That's enough,' Dad said.

I don't know why Lucy was so cross about me not believing her. Maybe she was still sore from where she said the dentist had jabbed her tongue.

'Bet you don't get chosen for your stupid camp anyway,' she hissed under her breath.

She was trying to wind me up but I wasn't bothered. 'Coach will choose the best players,' I said. 'And that means I'll be going to the training camp.'

CHAPTER ✿ FIVE

I was lying on the rug in the sitting room doing my homework the next day when Lucy came in pouting.

'That old lady called me a minx,' she said.

Ella was sitting at the table. She was doing her homework too, but in a much more tidy way. She put the lid on her pen and looked up at Lucy. 'Were you being naughty?'

Lucy rolled her eyes. 'Probably, but she still isn't allowed to call me names.'

'Do you even know what a minx is?' I asked.

'Of course I do! It's a big catty thing.'

'Well, the old lady is completely wrong there,' I said.

Lucy nodded. 'Exactly.'

'Because you're a tiny catty thing.'

'Hey!' Lucy flung herself on me with her elbow pointing down. It's called an elbow drop. Lucy always pays attention when I show her wrestling moves.

'Nice,' I said, pushing her off. 'But if you stick your elbow into my chubbiest parts it doesn't actually hurt that much.'

'Doesn't leave her with many options,' Amelia said, coming into the room and launching into a pirouette. 'Guess what?'

'What?' Ella asked, while I swept Lucy off her feet and grabbed her round the middle.

'I've found something Lauren can do!' Then she stopped. 'Actually, Ella found it because she's a lovely sister who is always thinking of other people.'

Ella blushed.

Lucy was turning pink too, but that was because I'd put her in a headlock. 'What did you find?' she panted to Amelia. 'Can I have some?'

'It's not something to eat,' Amelia said.

Lucy lost interest and went back to trying to wriggle herself free and claw my eyes out at the same time.

'Is it a choir?' I asked Amelia.

'Uh-huh, a community choir. Ella saw the poster when she was walking past the hall.'

'The one near Kayleigh's house,' Ella explained. 'Will Lauren's mum let her go?'

Amelia beamed. 'Yes! Because it's on a Sunday afternoon and I just rang the lady who runs it and I told her about Lauren and she said if she can't come one week because she's poorly that's completely fine; they're very relaxed and the whole point is for people to have fun.'

'That's great,' Ella said. 'I'm really pleased it's worked out.'

'What about me?' Lucy asked from my armpit.

I'd forgotten her for a moment. I relaxed my grip and since she was still straining to break loose she fell backwards and landed on her bum. 'There you go,' I said and I settled back down to my homework.

Lucy huffed. 'I didn't say I wanted you to stop! I'm bored. I want someone to play with.' She turned to Ella. 'Play with me.'

'Sorry, Lucy, I've got to do my homework and so has Chloe.'

Amelia eyed the circle of books and pens surrounding me. 'I don't know how you can get anything done sprawled out like that. Doesn't it make your writing all messy?'

'My writing's already all messy,' I said. 'Anyway, this way I can reach anything I need. I rolled over and grabbed a cushion. 'And in this position I can learn my French and be a thoroughbred racehorse for Lucy to win the Derby on.'

Lucy's eyes lit up.

I put the cushion on my back like a saddle and Lucy climbed on.

Amelia looked at Ella. She had ripped a tissue in half and was stuffing the pieces in her ears so she wouldn't have to listen to Lucy being a jockey.

'You're all mad,' Amelia said, though she was in such a good mood that she couldn't help smiling.

'But you love us,' I said. 'Look, Lucy, she's smiling a soppy smile of love. She loves us soooooo much.'

Ella was smiling to herself too.

Amelia pretended to be sick.

'You love us. You love us,' Lucy chanted as she started galloping away on her pretend horse race.

I concentrated on repeating my French vocabulary to the rhythm of her bouncing away on my poor back.

CHAPTER SIX

On Saturday morning, I was sitting on my bed, struggling into my rugby socks, when Amelia stopped snoring and opened half an eye to stare at me.

'Could you do that a bit more quietly?' she croaked.

'I'm putting on socks. I'm not banging cymbals together.'

'And yet somehow you manage to make a similar amount of noise.'

Amelia used to make grumpy sarcastic remarks like that all the time. Last year, she had a big heart-to-heart with my dad about my parents' divorce and since then she's been trying to be nicer to people. But she's not at her best early in the morning.

'How am I making a lot of noise?' I asked. 'Socks aren't noisy.'

She groaned. 'They are if you have to move your bed to find them and then you sing rugby songs while you're putting them on.'

She had a cheek complaining about my rugby songs. Amelia can't get down the stairs without blasting out a show tune. 'Don't get me started about people singing all the time.'

She pushed herself up on her elbows. 'At least I *can* sing!'

'Girls!' Mum called from the landing. 'Are you managing to have an argument before Amelia has even got out of bed?'

'Just friendly sisterly banter!' I called back.

'*We love each other really!*' Amelia sang in a really high-pitched voice.

'Yep,' I said, standing up. 'She loves my wrestling skills.' And I grabbed her legs from under the duvet and did a wrestling move on her called a figure-four that basically ties up your legs. She thrashed around a bit but, unlike Lucy, she's never really paid attention to any of the moves I've tried to teach her so she couldn't get out of it. I watched her squirm for a bit and then eventually I ruffled her hair and let her go.

She scowled. 'Just because you're scared about

seeing your coach, don't take your pent-up aggression out on me.'

That was a ridiculous thing to say because I don't get scared. Maybe I was feeling a teeny bit bad, like I'd let Coach down or something, but I absolutely wasn't afraid of what he was going to say to me. 'I'm not scared.'

'So you keep saying.'

I flopped down on the bed beside her. 'I just don't know why Coach didn't come and tell me off when he saw me.'

'He was probably feeling a bit unwell from seeing you flash your knickers when you jumped over that bin. The last time I had a good look at your pants I had to lie down for a while.'

My own insides were feeling a bit funny. 'I don't like waiting to hear what he's going to say. People should just come right out with what they think.'

'We all know that's the way you do it. Remember when you told Mrs Russell that she had a beard like a pirate?'

'I was only little! I didn't know I was being rude.'

'What's your excuse now you're the size of a baby elephant?'

I wasn't letting her get away with that. I knelt on her bed. 'Do you know what's good about baby elephants?'

I lunged towards her, but she realised what I was going to do and tried to hide under the covers. I grabbed hold of her, duvet and all, and hauled her onto my shoulder. 'The good thing about baby elephants is that they're really, really strong.'

'Stop it!' she growled. 'Put me down.'

'Strong enough to pick up their skinny elephant sisters and give them another look at the pants and socks that they're always going on about.'

'What? Chloe! Chloe, put me down.'

I'd got her through the door by then.

'What are you doing? I don't want to see any socks ... oh no! No, Chloe! Nooooooooo!' She was squealing like a pig. 'Chloe, CHLOE! I am serious, do not put me in the washing basket.'

It's quite hard carrying a teenage girl along a landing while she's waving her arms about, but I managed it. It's harder still to get her upside down with her head in a pile of dirty washing, but like my coach says: when you get a difficult job done you can feel really satisfied with yourself.

Even though Mum had a few things to say about not wanting her wicker washing basket to get broken and Amelia had a lot of things to say, including some quite rude words, I felt pretty pleased with myself. At least, I did until we got to rugby.

Coach didn't say anything to me at the beginning of training. I hoped that meant he wasn't cross with me. I decided to show him that I really do love rugby and I completely threw myself into the game. I might have thrown myself a bit too much because Coach did shout, 'Tackle her, don't kill her!' when I took Amirah down, but I think it just showed my enthusiasm.

When we were done, Coach beckoned me over. I gave him my most committed smile.

'Chloe,' he said. There was a big crease down the middle of his forehead and I hoped that meant he'd been thinking hard about how good I am. 'You're a powerful girl, but you've got to learn some control. Your passes are wild and you tackle like a drunken seaman.'

I grinned. 'My PE teacher says I'm powerful too.'

He shook his head like I'd misunderstood him.

'Powerful is good, isn't it?'

'Aye. But only if you use your power in the right places. You need accuracy and control. And to get there you'll need focused hard work.'

'I do work hard, look!' I lifted up my arms to show him the huge sweat rings on my shirt.

'It's not just sweating, lass, you have to use your brain too. Concentrate.'

I nodded.

'There's no doubt you've got talent, Chloe, but you'll have to settle down if you want to develop it.'

'I do.'

He gave me a long look. 'And if you do, you need to be here of a Saturday.'

I knew he was talking about me missing last week and those other times. I looked down at the muddy ground. 'I will be,' I said. 'Every Saturday. Honest.'

'And you'll take it seriously?'

'Definitely.'

He gave me another look as if he was measuring me with his eyes.

'I hope so,' he said. 'I hope after today you will.' And then he sent me to help the others collect up the equipment.

We were about to head into the scout hut where we get changed, but Coach clapped his hands and gathered us round him. Something was going on.

'I know you've all been waiting to hear who's been picked for the girls' training camp,' Coach said. 'So I've decided to put you out of your misery.'

A ripple went round the group. No one had expected to find out today.

Coach cleared his throat and went on. 'Remember that there are girls coming from all over the South West for this course, so I'm only allowed to recommend three lassies. Most of you have worked really hard this year and you've made great progress, but in the end I had to choose our most dedicated players with the greatest potential for progression.'

Amirah nudged me. I nudged her back. We're the team's star players.

'So, with all that in mind, the girls I've chosen are ... Lottie Fulbrook, Marta Blazowicz ...'

That was a surprise because it meant Amirah wasn't on the list.

'... and Io Etherington.'

Everything inside me dropped downwards as if I'd just shot up in a lift very fast. I didn't understand why Coach hadn't read my name out. I waited, but there were no more names. Amirah was muttering under her breath. I couldn't look at her.

Coach clamped his clipboard under his arm. 'This camp is a grand opportunity and I wanted to be sure the girls I picked would make the most of it. These three have turned up week after week and shown real grit so I'm sure they'll do us all proud.'

Several girls turned round to look at me. I stared straight ahead.

'If you've not been chosen for this camp,

remember there's always next time. Off you go and get changed and I'll see you all next week.'

I was first into the scout hut. There was no way I was hanging about getting changed so I just pulled off my boots and stuffed my feet into my trainers. I couldn't believe it. I wasn't going to be spending my half-term playing rugby every day. I wasn't going to get to challenge myself against the best players in our area. I wasn't going to have expert tuition from some of the top women players. I was going nowhere, and all because Coach didn't think I was good enough.

'This sucks,' Amirah said kicking her bag.

'I'm not bothered,' I lied. 'I might just go to the seaside at half-term anyway. I'll be eating ice cream on the beach while they're sweating it out and being all goody good and "disciplined".'

Amirah didn't say anything, but it was all over her face that she didn't believe me.

I bundled up my things and turned to go. I waved a hand round at everyone. 'See you,' I said as loudly and as don't care-ishly as I could.

A couple of them waved back. Lottie looked up and said, 'Oh, bye, Chloe, so sorry you're not coming to camp.' She pulled a soppy sympathetic face, but the sneery way she said *Chloe* made it clear she thought I was getting what I deserved.

I'm not like Lottie: I don't try and squeeze a nasty meaning into words that seem nice. I just say what I think. Except when I remember that Mum says that there is a third option, which is saying nothing, and sometimes that choice is the best way of keeping out of trouble. So instead of telling Lottie that she is a terrible rugby player and her breath smells of farts, I just walked out.

When I got home I told Mum what had happened. She gave me a hug, 'Maybe there'll be another camp in the summer,' she said, as if another camp could make up for the fact that Coach had basically called me rubbish in front of everyone.

'I wanted to go to this one.'

'I know, but Coach is in a difficult position, he can't choose everyone.'

I flopped down on the sofa and folded my arms over my face. I didn't care about him choosing everyone. I just wanted him to choose me.

CHAPTER ❤ SEVEN

Sunday was Amelia's first community choir session.

'Why don't you go too, Chloe?' Mum asked.

I turned to Amelia. She looked as horrified as I felt.

'I don't think that's a good idea,' I said.

'You've been moping around since you heard about rugby camp; I thought it might be something to amuse you.'

I didn't think it was fair to say I'd been moping. I was a bit sad and quite angry. That's a normal way to feel when your coach, who knows you're really good at rugby, has stopped you from going to rugby camp like you deserve.

Amelia grimaced. 'I know Chloe finds it amusing to make people suffer by listening to the honking noises that come out of her mouth, but

I'm not sure it would be fair on the other people at choir.'

'Yeah,' I said. 'Snooty singing snobs' – I pointed at Amelia – 'don't appreciate the unique quality my voice has. I should probably just stick to the shower and any time Amelia has friends over.'

'Or consider taking a vow of silence,' Amelia suggested.

'Are you sure you can't take your sister with you?' Mum asked. Her voice even sounded a little bit desperate. Anyone would think that she didn't enjoy having me around the house.

Just to prove to Mum that I wasn't a nuisance, while Amelia went off to do her silly singing, I kept myself totally amused by playing the recorder, doing somersaults on the sofa and making mustard-and-ketchup sandwiches. I'm really a very easy child to have around.

When Amelia got back I was lying on my bed throwing a tennis ball at the ceiling. 'How was your singing?' I asked.

'It's awesome. I love it. Lauren and I are practically the youngest ones there, but everybody treats us just like the adults.'

'Do you sing all that warbly stuff like you do in the school choir?'

'Nah, we sing all sorts. Today we did a folk song

and then two songs from a musical. And you're allowed to make suggestions if you like.'

'Imagine if I suggested some heavy metal to Mr Garcia.'

Mr Garcia is our super-strict music teacher.

Amelia snorted. 'It's completely different to school. I mean, don't get me wrong, I'm not one of those people who hates Mr Garcia because he's tough. I think it's good that he pushes us hard, but sometimes it's just nice to relax and enjoy singing.'

'Did Lauren like it?'

'Yeah. I think she's missed singing.' She picked up her hairbrush. Amelia brushes her hair eleventy-million times a day. It's amazing that she's got any left.

I threw the tennis ball at her head. Amelia managed to bat it away with her hairbrush and I caught it with one hand.

'Don't even think about throwing it again,' Amelia said.

I groaned. 'I'm so bored. I feel like one of those balloons when the air starts coming out and they get smaller and smaller until they're just a wrinkly little bit of rubber.'

Amelia turned up her nose. 'If you're going to pretend to be the remains of a balloon, can you please do it quietly? I've got to get started on my maths.'

So then I obviously had to pretend to be a

deflating balloon by blowing a loud raspberry and rushing around the room backwards. Amelia hit me over the head with a pillow so I sat on her and shouted, 'Who's queen of the balloons now?' That passed a bit of time, but then Amelia said she really did have to do her homework. I went to see what everybody else was doing. Mum was planning lessons. Ella was making notes for her Student Council meeting so that only left one person.

Lucy was out in the garden. She was standing on a deckchair next to the fence waving her hands about.

'. . . and then the curtain drops and you see the tiger in the cage and the magician has completely disappeared,' she said as I got closer.

'Oh, that one. I've seen that one,' said a voice from the other side of the fence. 'I can tell you how they do it if you like.'

'I already know,' Lucy said. 'I could *show* you how they do it.'

'Have you got a tiger, then?' The other voice said. I was close enough to see that it was the old lady from next door.

Lucy folded her arms. 'I might have. I've got a rabbit anyway.'

'Have you now? Doesn't sound quite as dramatic and dangerous as a tiger, does it?'

'Actually, he could give you a really hard bite. One day I'm going to let you hold him and then you'll find out.'

'Lucy!' I said. Everybody knows that you're not supposed to be rude to grown-ups and you're especially not supposed to be rude to the really old ones.

'What?' Lucy asked, turning round to face me and making the deckchair wobble. 'She said she was going to set her cat on me earlier.'

The cat was sitting on the old lady's lap. It was very fat and fluffy. I didn't think it would do much damage.

'I'm Chloe,' I said to the old lady.

'This is Mrs Grumpy-Pants,' Lucy said.

The old lady smiled at me. 'Don't take any notice of her. I'm Mrs Partridge. Your sister needs to wash her mouth out with soap.'

'If I need to, then so do you!' Lucy snapped. 'You called me Poo-see, earlier.'

I laughed. I was definitely going to save up that nickname to use later.

'What's that?' Mrs Partridge said, putting a hand to her ear. 'I can't hear.'

'She does that whenever she knows you're right,' said Lucy, still looking at Mrs Partridge.

Mrs Partridge ignored her. 'You must be the

sporty sister,' she said. 'I hear you're a very good jumper.'

'Yeah, jumping, running, all that stuff. I'm on a rugby team.' Then I remembered what happened yesterday and I felt a scrunch in my middle like someone was screwing up my insides like a ball of paper. 'Well, actually, I'm not that keen on rugby at the moment, but I play netball for my school sometimes.'

'Marvellous. I was very good at hockey. Best in my form. Best in the whole lower school, in fact.'

'She says that about everything,' Lucy said. 'Hockey's boring. Ballet's better.' And she did a flying leap off the deckchair and started twirling round the garden.

'Filthy little show-off,' Mrs Partridge said loudly, but she still watched Lucy throwing her arms and legs about.

We heard a door being opened and our neighbour, the boring man, came out into the garden. He screwed his eyes up against the sun and picked his way across the lawn as if he was afraid of the grass.

'Hello,' I said. 'It's a lovely day, isn't it?'

He made a 'hmm' noise while looking at Mrs Partridge.

If you do that when you're a child then you get

told to answer the question properly and speak up and look at the person you're talking to. But when you're a grown-up you get to decide which questions you think are worth answering. When I'm a grown-up I'm not going to answer any questions about science or when I last cut my toenails.

'Are these children bothering you, Mum?' Mr Partridge asked.

Mrs Partridge stroked her cat. 'Oh no. They're amusing me, aren't you, Lucy Poo-see?'

'Yes, Mrs *Fartridge*,' Lucy pulled a face, but I had a pretty good idea that she was enjoying herself just as much as Mrs Partridge. Lucy loves insults.

I didn't think Mr Partridge was a big fan. He looked at Lucy in quite a cross teacherish way and said, 'I see. Well, you'd better come in now, there's a bit of chill in the air.'

Mrs Partridge looked down at the cat. 'I'm fine.'

'Mother, I don't want you to get a cold.'

'Just ten more minutes.'

I was surprised to hear a grown-up talking like that. She sounded like Lucy trying to stay up a bit later.

'Five. And then you must come in and have a rest.'

He turned to go inside and Mrs Partridge and Lucy both stuck their tongues out at his back.

CHAPTER 🍓 EIGHT

Once the school week started I didn't think too much about missing out on rugby camp. There's no point getting upset about stuff you can't do anything about. But on Tuesday I had PE and as soon as we were out on the hockey field, Amirah came jogging over.

'I got a text from Lottie,' she said.

'Ugh. Was it a sad face? Did she tell you she was soooooo sorry you haven't been chosen?'

'Oh, she wasn't pretending to be nice, she just got straight to the bad news.'

'What bad news?'

'She reckons there are going to be England players at the camp.'

My mouth fell open. 'Actual players from the women's England rugby team?'

'Uh-huh.'

I couldn't believe it. I knew there would be professional players at the camp but I'd never thought it would be England players. I was going to miss out on meeting my heroes and instead Lottie idiot-face was going to get to talk to them. 'Are they going to be coaching?' I asked.

'That's what she said.'

We stared at each other. Imagine meeting the England captain. I bet she could give me some brilliant tips. My scalp was hot and prickly. If Lottie had been there I think I might have punched her.

'This is so unfair,' Amirah said. 'We should be going to that camp. Coach is punishing us and there's absolutely nothing we can do about it.'

I was so mad that when Mrs Henderson blew her whistle to start, I absolutely flew around the pitch. I couldn't understand why Coach was doing this to me. I was the best at rugby, so how come I didn't get to meet the England players? It was ridiculous and mean and stupid. I wasn't going to let him treat me like this. The next time I ran past Amirah, I called over to her, 'You're wrong, you know. There is something we can do.' I gripped my hockey stick harder. 'And I'm going to do it.'

*

'It's just one camp,' Ella said, when we were walking home with Amelia. 'I know you're sad about it, but you can still enjoy playing rugby.'

'How am I supposed to enjoy it when I know that Coach thinks I'm useless?'

'He didn't say that, did he?'

'Not exactly, but the camp is for the best three and he hasn't chosen me, has he? So it's pretty obvious.' Coach had been totally unfair. He didn't seem to care that he was taking away something I really, really wanted. He was completely ignoring the fact that it was me who had got the club to run girls' training sessions in the first place. It ought to be me going to that camp. I deserved to meet the England players.

'I thought he didn't choose you because he thought you weren't reliable enough,' Amelia said. 'You could show him that you can be reliable and turn up to roll around in the mud every week instead of skiving off to go rolling around in the mud somewhere else.'

'It's no good me showing up all the time now, I've already been left out of the training camp and now I won't get to meet the England players.'

Amelia shrugged. She doesn't really understand people getting excited about sports.

Ella squeezed my elbow. 'I think your coach

knows you're a good player,' she said gently. 'You're normally in all the matches, aren't you?'

But who cared about little local matches? At camp Lottie, Marta and Io were going to get to train with some of the best girls in the country.

'And you're always winning your matches,' Ella said.

I wasn't interested in her trying to cheer me up. 'Yeah, well, let's see how many of those they win without me,' I said.

'What do you mean?' Ella asked.

'I'm quitting.'

Ella gasped. Even Amelia looked surprised. Which was sort of satisfying because so far no one had really seemed to care how mad I was. And I was mad. Much madder than I'd even realised. This was unfair and I wasn't going to pretend everything was all right.

'You can't just give up stuff,' Ella said.

'Why not?' I'd show Coach he couldn't do this to me. He couldn't treat his best player this way and expect me to just carry on like nothing had happened.

Ella struggled to get her words out. 'Because . . . it's a commitment . . . and, I don't know, you have to . . . You have to stick to things.'

'No I don't.' Then I realised that it wasn't just

rugby that she thought you had to keep on at even if you were miserable. 'And you don't either. I'm quitting rugby and you can quit Student Council.'

Ella pressed her lips together and I knew I wouldn't be able to persuade her. But now that I'd made my own decision I was determined to go through with it.

That night I had a long and boring talk with Mum all about it and the next night when we went to Dad's I had to have a short and boring talk with Dad. (I thought it was going to be a long one, but Kirsti's nappy started leaking part way through and after Dad had peeled a pooey Babygro off her and washed her pooey legs I think he was tired out. I'm glad that at least one sister is on my side.) When I finally convinced him that nothing was going to change my mind, Dad still insisted I'd have to tell Coach in person. I think he thought the idea of having to explain would make me back down, but I didn't care what that mean old man thought about me, so Dad put Kirsti in her bouncy chair where Suvi could keep an eye on her while she was making tea, and drove me down to Langley Fields where Coach was running his under-tens session.

I waited till the kids were busy practising their kicks with partners and I went over.

'Hullo, Chloe!' Coach said when he saw me.

He sounded pleased to see me. It would have been easier if he'd seemed all stern and disappointed like he had on Saturday, but I wasn't going to forget that he'd cheated me out of being coached by England players just because he was smiling.

'Hi,' I said. 'I've just come to tell you that I'm quitting rugby.'

He blinked. 'Quitting?'

'I'm not coming to training any more.'

He was quiet for a moment. I had thought that he might launch into one of his rants and tell me that I was ungrateful, after all I was the one who had worked so hard last year to get the girls' squad set up, and now here I was turning my back on it. Actually, I guess what I had really been hoping was that he would ask me not to leave; maybe even tell me that if I stayed, he would put me on the list for camp, but he didn't say any of that. Instead, he said, 'That's a shame.'

He looked quite sad.

And I felt quite sad because suddenly it seemed like I wasn't going to be playing rugby any more, which is not at all what I thought was going to happen. I could feel a bubble of sadness expanding inside me and I wanted to make it stop, but when you say something you have to stick by it and I couldn't back down so I said, 'I think I need to concentrate on other sports.'

There was another long pause.

'Well, we've enjoyed having you on the squad, Chloe. If you find you've more time in future we'd be pleased to see you again.'

I didn't know what to say. I was horrified that my rugby playing seemed to be disappearing into the future. I felt like you do when you wake up on Boxing Day and all the fun is over. It seemed like nothing nice would ever happen again. I wished I could teleport myself home and under my duvet, but I managed to say, 'Well, bye, then.'

'Goodbye, lass.' And he turned back to the kids.

I had to go and get back in the car with Dad. I didn't want to admit to him that things hadn't gone the way I wanted. I'd said I was going to quit and that was what had happened.

'How did it go?' Dad asked.

'Fine. Yep, fine.'

'Was he cross?'

'No, not cross. He was fine.' I blinked a bit. 'It's all fine.'

And he hadn't been cross. I always thought that someone telling you off and shouting at you is the worst thing, but I was starting to think that it's actually more upsetting when someone is just really disappointed in you.

CHAPTER ❦ NINE

The next day I felt a bit flat. Then I decided that I was being stupid. Rugby isn't the only thing in the world and I'm very good at thinking up things to do to entertain myself, so after school I made a brilliant obstacle course all over the house until Mum and Lucy got back and Mum looked at the course and said, 'What's all this, Chloe?'

When I looked at it, I had got rather a lot of stuff out. 'It's an obstacle course,' I said.

'Goodness, I tend to find that there are enough obstacles when I'm trying to get from one end of this house to the other as it is. Can you pack it up before tea, please?'

I don't really see the point of tidying up. It seemed a shame to pack it away when I might feel like having another go later. But Mum cares about tidying stuff up, especially things on the stairs, because she worries that if there's a fire in the middle of the night we'll all trip and fall and break our ankles. I've told her that we're more likely to die in our sleep from breathing the smoke in, but that doesn't seem to make her feel any better.

I cleared the stairs first. Then I took down the badminton net from where it was stretched across the hall and took it outside to put it back in the shed.

Lucy was in the garden, standing on the deckchair again.

'Why are you always out here?' Lucy asked Mrs Partridge.

'Well, it's not for your polite conversation, is it?' They both cackled like witches about that.

'I've always liked gardens,' Mrs Partridge said, rearranging her cushion behind her back. 'When I was a little girl, we didn't have a garden, but my dad did have an allotment and he let me have one corner of it and I grew such lovely flowers there. I was so proud of them. When James Somerfield tried to pick some of my tulips I kicked him in the shins.'

They laughed again. Mrs Partridge seemed to like violence as much as Lucy. I had to rattle the shed door a bit to get it open, but neither of them was paying any attention to me.

'Then one day my poor mum got pneumonia and she was stuck in our flat for days on end with nothing but the walls to look at. So I cut all my flowers and put them in her bedroom.'

I chucked the badminton net into the shed and closed the door again.

'What did you do that for?' Lucy asked Mrs Partridge.

'To cheer her up.'

'But they were your flowers.'

'Yes. Mine to do what I wanted to do with them. And I wanted to cheer up my mum.'

'I come out in the garden because I like the digging,' Lucy said, completely changing the subject.

'I used to like that too. Bit harder now with my hands.'

I'd opened the kitchen door to go back inside but I turned round to see Mrs Partridge holding up her hands; the fingers were curled over as if she couldn't straighten them out.

'They're like claws,' Lucy said.

I sucked in my breath at that. I didn't know what old lady thing had made Mrs Partridge's hands like that, but I did know that it's the sort of thing you're supposed to pretend you haven't noticed. Mrs Partridge didn't seem to mind; she just stretched out a hand towards Lucy's face and said, 'All the better for scratching little girls' eyes out with.'

I left them to it.

In the kitchen, Mum was chopping salad.

'Do you think you should tell Lucy she can't talk to Mrs Partridge any more?' I asked.

Mum looked up. 'What makes you say that? She hasn't done anything awful, has she?'

I thought about it. 'Not *awful* awful, but she's pretty rude.'

She pulled the greeny bit off the top of a tomato. 'Yes, I've heard them.'

'Aren't you going to tell her off?'

There were more shouts of laughter from the garden.

Mum smiled. 'Mrs Partridge gives as good as she gets. I think she quite enjoys squabbling with your little sister.'

It was true that Mrs Partridge hadn't seemed bothered by anything Lucy said. In fact, they were laughing so much she must be finding it funny. Somehow I didn't expect an old person to have that sort of sense of humour.

'It is quite fun being rude to each other,' I said.

'It's certainly your favourite way to spend time with Amelia.'

I nodded. 'That's true. Except Amelia and I usually finish things with an arm wrestle.' I stole a slice of cucumber. 'You'd better tell Lucy not to try that; old people's bones break really easily.'

CHAPTER ✦ TEN

It was brilliant not having to get up really early on Saturday to go to rugby. I mean, I couldn't help thinking about the girls and wondering if they would miss me, but at least when I woke up at the usual time I got to snuggle into the duvet and go back to sleep. The problem is that I'm not really a very sleepy person, so half an hour later, I was completely awake and I thought I might as well get up.

I played with Kirsti who was already awake, along with Suvi. Then I had some breakfast. Then I read a graphic novel Thunder lent me. Then I had some more breakfast. By the time Amelia came downstairs I was ready for some company. I sat down beside her at the kitchen table where she was chewing toast.

'I'm bored,' I said.

'I knew you would be. Do you know how I knew? Because you're like one of those puppies that needs loads of exercise or it starts chewing up slippers and peeing on the carpet. I knew it was a bad idea for you to quit rugby. I knew you'd be like this.'

It was true that my Saturday was looking very long now that I didn't have anything to do all morning. There was a sinking feeling in my stomach. Was every Saturday going to be like this from now on? I sighed. 'Well, I am. I'm sooooo bored.'

'And your plan to get un-bored is to keep repeating the same phrase to someone who only half-listens to you even when you've actually got something to say? Good luck with that.'

'I just wish I had something to do.'

'Why do you always have to do stuff? Why don't you just relax? You could read a book or have a conversation with someone. Someone who isn't me. I'm going to meet Milly and Jasveen in a minute.'

I pinched a triangle of her toast. 'Talking doesn't really interest me that much.'

'That's funny because you do it all day long. Even when it's just to tell us what's come out of your nose.'

'Yeah, but doing stuff is better.'

Amelia licked some jam off her finger. 'Do you really think that? I love just sitting around having a good chat.'

I tried to work out exactly what the problem with chatting was. 'When you talk it's just sort of thinking out loud about what you've done or what you could do and what it would be like.'

'So?'

'So that's okay, but when you *do* a thing, you're feeling it.' I thought about how they'd be playing a practice match at training right now. 'You're right in the middle of something, using your body and your mind and you don't even have time to worry about all the little details because it's going on right now and you're there, and you've got the wind in your face and your heart is pumping and things are *happening*.'

Amelia stared at me. 'When you talk like that it does sort of make me want to go out and do something. But you're not talking about skydiving or trekking through the jungle, are you? You mean rolling about with a rugby ball.'

She was totally missing the point of how exciting rugby can be. I drew myself up tall. 'It's not just rolling about. It's working as a team with your mates and pushing yourself to your limits and struggling and fighting and gasping for breath until you claw your way to victory.' I slumped forward in my chair. 'Oh, man, I really miss it.'

'Then you shouldn't have quit, should you?'

I sort of wished I hadn't. 'Coach wasn't being fair. I don't see why I should miss out on fun because of him.'

She stood up. 'You've got to make your own fun. You used to be good at making up games. Why don't you play with Ella and Lucy?'

Then she went off in a swirl of hair and perfume to meet her friends.

She had a good point about making things up. There was no reason why I couldn't think of something fun to do. And it didn't have to be with Ella and Lucy; I could ring Thunder and Amirah. What could we do? I really fancied skydiving now that Amelia had mentioned it, but I knew that would be hard to sort out and probably too expensive anyway. I liked the idea of wind in my hair and my heart pounding and all that. There had to be something we could do that would get our hearts racing. I made myself one last breakfast and sat down to think about it.

That's when I thought of the Ghost School.

*

I arranged to meet Thunder and Amirah at the park after lunch so I could tell them my brilliant idea about the Ghost School. Actually, it had started off just about the Ghost School but then I'd decided to make it even bigger than that.

Thunder asked me if he could bring Riley from our class and I said yes because I quite like him and because I was pretty sure that he was the kind of person who would think my brilliant idea *was* brilliant, rather than going and telling a grown-up about it and spoiling the whole thing.

They were all sitting on the swings when I arrived.

'How was training this morning?' I asked Amirah. I was just asking to be polite. Obviously I wasn't actually bothered about how they were getting on without me.

'I don't know,' Amirah said. 'I didn't go because I've quit too.'

I was pretty surprised by that. I guess I'd thought that I was more upset about the whole thing than Amirah was, but when I remembered her furious face when she told me about the England players it did make sense. I supposed it was a good thing because Coach would definitely miss good players like me and Amirah and he might realise that he should never have left us out of training camp, but

I'd sort of been looking forward to Amirah filling me in on what was happening with the squad.

Amirah snapped her fingers at me. 'Forget about that, what's this big secret?'

I settled myself on a swing. 'Well, I've been getting pretty bored since I stopped rugby.'

'Stop going on about rugby, you've only not been doing it for five minutes,' Amirah said.

'All right, all right, it's just weird not having anything to do on Saturdays.' This wasn't going the way I'd planned it. 'Anyway, I was thinking we should do something.'

'That's a great idea!' Thunder said.

Amirah looked sideways at him. 'She hasn't actually told us the idea yet.'

'Oh. Right. Go on then, Chloe.'

I clicked my knuckles. 'I want to start something. I want to have a good time without anyone saying I'm not allowed to make jokes or that I'm rubbish at rugby.'

'He didn't actually say that,' Amirah interrupted.

'He didn't say I could go to camp either, did he?'

She folded her arms. 'Are you going to tell us what the big idea is or are you just going to cry about being left off Coach's list?'

Amirah was right, I was getting sidetracked. 'Okay, okay. It's called . . .' I paused like they do on the TV before they tell you who's been voted out. '. . . Adrenaline Club!'

Riley looked confused. I mean, he always looks confused, but now his whole face crumpled like he was trying to understand one of those crazy diagrams that Mr Chadwick draws on the whiteboard. 'A club? Like at primary school?'

I shook my head. 'Not like primary school. We're going to be a secret society that do dares that will give us an adrenaline rush. We take it in turns to think up dares for the others and if anyone fails to do it then they're out of the club.'

'That's a great idea!' Thunder said. I think he might have said that if I'd suggested we all have a sandwich. I love the way Thunder is always up for everything.

Amirah was pretending she wasn't interested but she couldn't stop herself from saying, 'What kind of dares?'

I grinned. 'Dangerous ones.'

'Do you mean like climbing up really high and stuff?' Riley asked.

'Could be, or it could be something that might get you into trouble if you get caught.'

Riley gave a tiny nod like maybe he was just starting to get a little bit of an idea about what it was all about. Thunder was beaming and even

Amirah, who usually likes picking holes in other people's plans, hadn't said it was a stupid idea, so I was feeling pretty pleased.

'Are you all in then?' I asked.

'Definitely,' Thunder said.

'Yep,' Riley said.

Amirah chewed a fingernail. 'I suppose so. I haven't got anything better to do.'

'Good. I'll give the first dare because it was my idea.'

They were all sitting completely still, waiting to hear what I said. It was brilliant. I love being in charge. 'This week,' I said. 'After dark, we're going to gather under the Headmistress's Tree at the Ghost School.'

Thunder's eyes bulged. 'But that place is haunted!'

'That's the point!' Riley said. He was getting the hang of it now. 'That's why it's a dare.'

'There's no such thing as ghosts,' Amirah said.

'Aren't you coming, then?' I asked.

'I'll come. But when it's my turn to choose a challenge I'm going to think up something properly scary.'

'Good,' I said. 'I can't wait.'

CHAPTER ❧ ELEVEN

When Mum came home on Tuesday she insisted that while she was cooking tea, we all went down to the Pit to give it what she called a quick 'going over'. So we trudged downstairs to our playroom. Amelia gets annoyed with me when I call it the playroom because she says it's babyish, but mostly we call it the Pit anyway because it's in the basement and it looks like a troll's pit. No matter how much tidying up we do, it's always covered in toys and books. In fact, if it was just toys and books it wouldn't look so bad, but there are also crisp packets and screwed-up letters from school, apple cores and dirty socks, crusty cereal bowls and bits of dried Play-Doh.

'Ugh,' Amelia said, picking up a mug with a sort of brown slime in the bottom. 'You can pick up anything food related,' she said to me. 'Because it's bound to have been you who left it there in the first place.'

'That makes no sense,' I said. 'When I have a snack or a drink I never leave any of it behind.' But I started collecting cups anyway.

'And you can wipe up that sticky stuff on the table,' Amelia said to Lucy.

Lucy flopped down on a cushion. 'Do it yourself; I'm not your tweenie.'

When we were younger we used to play this game called Tweenie. In Year Six Amelia did a project on the Victorians and she learnt all about the servants they used to have in big houses. If you were rich you had a whole team of them and they all had different names like parlour maid (who kept the parlour tidy) and kitchen maid and dairy maid and probably picks-up-your-knickers maid as well. But the type of maid that we liked best was one that worked for less rich people and had to do a mixture of jobs, like tidying upstairs and downstairs, so she was called a between maid, or a tweenie, for short. Amelia made up this game where she was a Victorian lady in one of Mum's long skirts and I was the butler (in Dad's best black shiny shoes) and Ella and Lucy were tweenies. Basically Amelia spent the whole time swishing her skirt and bossing people about.

You can see why she liked that game so much.

Sometimes she even made us tidy her half of the bedroom. Ella never minded because she liked pretending she was Victorian and even used to do curtseys. But Lucy used to shout at Lady Amelia and tell her that her posh voice sounded like a horse having its tail pulled out.

She wasn't a very good servant.

'Come on, Lucy,' I said, giving her a poke with my foot. 'We've all got to tidy.'

'I am! I'm doing it with my feet.' Very slowly she managed to pull a teddy towards her with her toes.

Amelia tutted. 'You could try using the rest of you. Look at Ella.'

Ella had completely cleared one corner. She was working her way methodically along, picking up everything. She had a stack of books and papers and was scooping Lucy's toys into one of those plastic baskets.

'I need my top half for thinking,' Lucy whined.

I opened the cupboard and slid the Monopoly box onto the shelf. 'What are you thinking about?'

'I want to do something nice for Mrs Fartridge.'

'If you want to be nice, you could stop calling her names,' Ella suggested.

'I don't think that's a good idea, Ella,' Amelia said. 'We don't want her to think that Lucy is ill.'

I could see Lucy was wondering if it was worth getting up off her comfy cushions to wallop Amelia so I said, 'You could give her a present.'

'Maybe,' Lucy said suspiciously. 'Like what?'

'I don't know. What does she like?'

'She likes magic tricks and gardening.'

I looked at Ella. 'Those sorts of things aren't the kind of stuff you can wrap up as a present.'

Amelia crammed a stack of magazines under the sofa. 'How about a scarf? Old people like woolly stuff.'

Lucy shook her head. 'It will be summer soon.'

'I don't think they care about that,' I said. 'Granny wears cardigans even when they go to Spain.'

Amelia pulled one of the magazines back out and flicked it open. 'When you give a present you have to think really hard about what someone wants. Remember at Christmas when I decorated Lauren's room?'

'Hmm,' I said to Ella and Lucy. 'Do you remember at Christmas when Amelia painted Lauren's room? And it was all her own idea and it was completely brilliant and we had to listen to Amelia going on about it for hours and hours?'

Ella was trying not to crack up. She thinks it's unkind to laugh at people, but you can't fight the truth.

'Ella? Lucy?' I said again. 'Remember? Lauren's room? Remember Amelia, the angel who walks among us?'

'I remember,' Lucy said. 'Do you remember, Ella? Amelia, the most perfectest friend ever?'

Ella spluttered. 'I think I remember something about it.'

Amelia gave me the stink eye. 'Yeah, yeah,' she said. 'I'm just trying to help Lucy do something thoughtful.' She turned to Lucy. 'Try to think of something that she's always wanted.'

Lucy screwed up her face in concentration, but she couldn't think of anything.

I think she must have kept on thinking about it, though, because she wasn't much help tidying the Pit and she didn't say much at tea.

When I went to clean my teeth before bed, Lucy was in the bathroom dangling an upside-down Barbie over the loo.

'What are you doing?' I asked.

'She's the one with the code to the missiles that will hit earth in thirty-seven seconds. She won't talk.'

'You're not going to scare her with toilet water.

Barbies float. You'd be better off threatening her with a microwave than a toilet bowl.'

Lucy hauled Barbie up and sat on the side of the bath. 'I've thought of something that Mrs Partridge always wanted.'

I squeezed toothpaste onto my brush. 'What's that?'

'Money. She told me. She always wanted to be rich.'

I never really think about money. I supposed it would be cool if you had enough to buy a quad bike. Or a giant bar of Dairy Milk. 'There's not much you can do about that,' I said, 'because you're not rich, are you?'

Lucy dug one of Barbie's feet into the soap. 'I've got twenty-three pounds and seventy-two pence in my money box,' she said huffily. 'And anyway I wasn't talking about just that money, I mean I'm going to make money to give to her. Lots of money. Loads. So she'll actually be rich.'

'How much money?' I asked.

'One hundred pounds.' She said it in the kind of voice that a game show host uses when he's talking about a million dollars. And she looked up at me to see what I thought.

I knew that I should probably tell her that it's quite hard to make money and that Mum might not let her and that even if she did make a hundred pounds it wouldn't exactly make Mrs Partridge rich, but when I looked at her face, I remembered what it was like to be quite small and to really want to do something that everyone else thinks is stupid, so instead I said, 'You could have a cake stall.'

The problem with being a kid is that whenever you have an excellent idea, some grown-up comes along and tells you it's not excellent at all. They say it's *impractical* or *too difficult* or even *irresponsible and downright dangerous*. This is why sometimes I keep my plans quiet, but Lucy always thinks people will think all her ideas are wonderful, so the next day at breakfast she announced her cake-stall plans to Mum.

Mum frowned, which is the first sign that an adult can't see what's so brilliant about your plan, then she said, 'Where are you planning on selling these cakes exactly?' (Asking a load of questions is the next sign.)

Lucy looked a bit surprised. As if she'd just expected people to turn up at our house with their pockets loaded with cash. 'Outside,' she said finally. 'By the road.'

Mum's face clouded. 'I don't think you'll get much custom that way,' she said. 'And I don't really want you bothering anyone.'

By this point I was pretty sure that the whole thing was off, but Lucy never admits defeat.

'I'm not going to bother anyone,' she said. 'They do it on TV all the time. They have lemonade stands like the one in the duck song and people give them money.'

'That's in America,' I pointed out.

Lucy sighed. 'I wish I was in America. They get to go to Disneyland and they don't have school uniform and they eat peanut butter with jelly.'

'It's not really jelly,' I said. 'That's what Americans call jam.'

Lucy crossed her eyes. 'Why would anyone want to eat peanut butter with jam?'

'Why would anyone want to eat it with jelly?' Mum asked.

Lucy leant back in her chair and stuck her legs in the air. '*I* would. Imagine what it would be like in your mouth! Especially if it was crunchy peanut butter. It would be amazing. Slippery *and* sticky.'

'I like peanut butter with Marmite,' I said, but no one was listening to me.

Mum leant to one side to avoid Lucy's slipper flying off her kicking foot. 'Back to this cake idea. How would you like to sell your cakes at my school fair?'

Lucy stopped kicking. 'I wouldn't like it at all.'

'Why not?' Mum asked.

'Because this is my thing. I don't want there to be other people there.'

'You need the other people to buy the cakes, you banana!' I said. 'Anyway, Mum, isn't the fair supposed to make money for your school?'

'It is, but if Lucy does all the cooking and helps to sell the cakes it will save me a lot of bother and I will pay her five pounds.'

Lucy pouted. 'Is that all?'

I could see Mum was starting to get annoyed. 'Don't be so grabby, Lucy Strawberry!' she said. 'Really, I don't think it would be asking too much if I said I wanted you to help your poor mother for free.'

'Fine. I'll take the five pounds,' Lucy said, as if she was doing Mum a huge favour.

'Of course, you're going to need some supervision, if you're going to be baking.' Mum looked at me and then over at Amelia, who had just stumbled into the kitchen and was groping about in the cereal cupboard. I know that look. It's when she expects me and Amelia to be good, unselfish big sisters and to help out. I don't know why she keeps expecting it; you'd think she hadn't met me and Amelia. There was a long silence. 'I can't do it,' Amelia said. 'I promised to help Lauren catch up on what she's missed in biology on Saturday.'

'Well, I can't do it either,' I said. 'I've got ...' Then I realised I hadn't got any rugby training to use as an excuse. And I also realised that we were talking about cakes here. 'Oh, all right,' I said. 'I'll do it. But I'm warning you, I'm going to have to taste these cakes to make sure they're nice.'

'Of course,' said Mum. 'That's admirable attention to detail.'

CHAPTER ❦ TWELVE

In stories, kids can always manage to sneak out of their houses after dark and go off and have adventures and get held hostage and then escape and stop the diamond smugglers and somehow get back home in time for breakfast without their parents even noticing. In my house, if you get out of bed in the night to get a drink of water it sets off my mum's spidey sense and she's there in her nighty feeling your forehead and asking if you think you're going to be sick. So I knew that I had to think carefully about when the Adrenaline Club should meet at the Headmistress's Tree. Everyone knows that the proper time to visit a creepy place is at midnight, but obviously there was no way we could manage that, so in the end we agreed to meet at seven forty-five when the sun would be going down. Even then, I had to promise Mum that I would be back before nine.

I called for Thunder on the way there and when we arrived outside the Ghost School, Amirah and Riley were waiting for us.

Amirah peered through the gates. It was still just about light. The paint was peeling off the school sign but other than that everything looked quite normal.

'This dare isn't very scary,' Amirah said.

I frowned at her. 'Wait till we get under the tree.'

'Let's go,' Thunder said, and he grabbed hold of the gate like he was about to swing himself over it.

'Not here!' I said, pulling him away. 'We need to go through the park and over the back fence. There are too many houses around this way in.'

So we went down the alleyway that leads into the park. As we got further away from the road the traffic noise faded. There are no lights in the park and it was completely deserted. Thunder was going on about Mr Chadwick and how he'd made him stay in at breaktime just because he dropped his pencil case, but once he stopped talking all we could hear were our own feet padding across the grass.

'This is it,' I said.

We looked at the fence. It was one of those wire ones with diamond-shaped holes. It wasn't much taller than me.

Thunder bent his knees and laced his fingers together. 'I'll give you a bunk up,' he said to me.

Just for a second, I didn't move. I was a bit surprised that we'd made it this far. I'd sort of expected something to happen to stop us, or for one of the others to chicken out. I looked round at them. They were all just waiting for me to climb over the fence.

So I did.

Thunder boosted me up and I swung my leg over and then there I was in the grounds of the Ghost School. The others followed pretty easily, although the fence did sag horribly when Thunder hauled himself over it.

'Now what?' Riley asked.

I pointed across the grass to the school building itself. When we reached it, Thunder got a torch out of his pocket and we all pressed our faces against the window while he pointed the beam so we could get a look inside. I'd thought it would be completely empty, but we could see some of those low-down tables and chairs that reception children use. There were even pictures and photos stuck up on the walls. It was amazing to think how this cobwebby place was once full of little kids painting and singing and eating their school dinner. Now it was so old and still.

'Where's the tree?' Amirah asked.

'This way,' I said. Even though I didn't really know where I was going.

But as soon as we got round the corner it was obvious which tree we wanted. There was just one at the edge of a tarmacked play area. We made our way towards it and once again I realised how quiet it was. The sun had dipped right out of sight by now and it was pretty shadowy. We stared through the dusk at the tree.

At first, I was a bit disappointed.

I'd been thinking about this tree for so long that in my imagination, it had turned into something terrifying. In my head, it was massive and black with razor-sharp twigs and twisted roots snaking across the ground. Now I was standing in front of it, I could see it was just an ordinary tree.

I looked at the others. They didn't seem disappointed. Amirah's sneery face had finally disappeared. Thunder had pulled the sleeves of his fleece down over his hands and was chewing one of the cuffs. Riley was staring up at the branches. That's when I realised that if I wanted to, I could make this ordinary tree pretty creepy. I could make the hairs stand up on the back of their necks.

'This is the Headmistress's Tree,' I said in a low voice. 'Every year, delicious red apples grew on it. But every child in the school, even the babies in reception, knew that the apples were only to be eaten by the headmistress. If you ate one she would curse you. But there was one child, a girl—'

'I heard it was a boy,' Thunder interrupted. 'A boy called John.'

When I tell stories, the girl gets the main part so I ignored him and went on. 'A girl called . . . Jen. She had had enough of the headmistress. She was fed up with her always telling her off for mucking about and making people laugh. Then one day the headmistress kicked Jen out of the netball team, even though everybody knew that Jen was the best player . . .'

Amirah raised her eyebrows. I was getting a bit sidetracked.

'Anyway, Jen decided she was going to pay the headmistress back: she was going to have one of those precious apples. So the next playtime, she climbed into the tree and picked an apple—' I paused for what Amelia calls 'dramatic effect' – 'but at the very moment that she took a bite the headmistress appeared at the window and shouted,

"*Get down!*" Jen didn't get down. She just stuck out her tongue and said, "I didn't want to be on your stupid team anyway." The headmistress stared at Jen and her eyes went all creepy and black, "I said *Get Down!*" And she lifted up her hand like this . . .' I raised my right hand slowly. 'And Jen finally did get down because the headmistress cursed her and Jen was thrown out of the apple tree . . .'

We all looked up at the spindly top of the tree.

'. . . and smashed against the hard playground and broke her neck.'

Thunder swallowed so loudly that I heard him.

'The headmistress was taken away to prison and they closed the school down. But if anyone dares to take an apple then the ghost of Jen appears and chokes them with it.'

Riley let out a long shuddery breath.

'Hey, what's this?' I pretended to see something in the grass

'What?' Amirah asked.

'Looks like an apple.' I bent down and stretched out a hand as if I was going to pick it up.

Amirah gasped.

'No!' Thunder shouted.

Riley gave me one horrified look and turned and ran back to the fence.

Thunder grabbed hold of my hood and yanked me backwards. 'Run!' he said, and he gripped me by the elbow and dragged me away. He didn't let go till he'd half-thrown me over the fence. Then he pushed me all the way back across the park until we were outside the gates and standing under a streetlight. We were all panting for breath.

Riley looked like he might be sick. 'Did you pick up the apple?' he asked.

I widened my eyes and hesitated just for a moment. '. . . Nah.'

We burst out laughing. I think Thunder was a bit hysterical.

'I reckon I saw something,' Riley said. 'There was something in that tree, something white, like a school shirt.'

Thunder shuddered and went off into giggles again.

I looked at Amirah. 'What do you think of my dare now?'

She pushed up her sleeve to show me her arm. There were definitely goosebumps on it. 'Not bad,' she said. 'Not bad at all.'

CHAPTER ✦ THIRTEEN

It was quite nice when I woke up on Saturday morning this week because even though there was no rugby I did have something to do. Plus, there was still a nice swooshing feeling in my middle every time I thought about Adrenaline Club and the Ghost School. I ate my breakfast and then went into Ella and Lucy's bedroom and pulled Lucy's duvet off her.

'Wha' izit?' she said sleepily.

'Time to get up,' I said. 'We need to get started on these cakes. They need to be at the fair at two o'clock.'

She tried to pull the duvet back. 'I've got ballet.'

'That doesn't start for ages.'

There was even more moaning when she worked out that I'd woken her earlier than she has to get up for school. But in the end, I managed to get her into some clothes and down to the kitchen.

I pulled the mixing bowl out of the cupboard.

'I'll get my plans,' Lucy said.

'What plans?'

'I did some plans of what to make.'

And she had. She'd filled up half an old exercise book with elaborate drawings of five-tier cakes.

'It's a cake stall, not a wedding,' I pointed out.

'So? That doesn't mean we can't make nice cakes.'

I was already starting to regret agreeing to help. 'I don't even know how to make cakes like this.'

'It's easy,' Lucy said. Even though she knows nothing about cooking. 'You just keep piling them up on top of each other. And then you ice them. I thought I might make an icing swan like they did on TV.'

I slapped a bag of flour down on the counter. 'We're not making that gigantic cake.'

'Yes, we are.'

'I say we're not and I'm the only one who's allowed to touch the cooker, so you're going to have to make the cakes I say.'

Her eyes flicked about as she thought hard. I bet she even considered pushing raw cake on the poor school fair people but in the end it was obvious she had no choice.

'What do you want to do then?' she asked, sticking out her bottom lip.

I rolled up my sleeves. 'I thought we'd do a big thing of brownies that we can cut into little squares and then lots and lots of fairy cakes.'

'Is that all? We need something big and fancy to put in the middle of the table.'

I ran through all the cakes I'd ever made in my life. There weren't that many. 'I suppose we could do a Victoria sponge.'

'And I can put a swan on top of it.'

'Okay,' I said. I was pretty sure that by the time we'd done everything else Lucy would have forgotten all about the swan.

We started with the fairy cakes.

'We need hundreds and hundreds,' Lucy said.

'Well, we've only got two twelve-hole tins so that's . . .'

'Twenty-four,' Lucy interrupted.

'I knew that. And we could do two batches so . . .'

'Forty-eight.'

'Yes, forty-eight.' I looked at the recipe. 'This says it makes sixteen. We'll need more mixture than that. If we double it then . . .' I chewed my cheek. Double wouldn't be enough. But double and double again would be way too much, wouldn't it? 'Maybe we should just add more of everything.'

Lucy scowled. 'You can't just make it up. It's not just for you to eat, it has to actually be nice. Do the recipe properly.'

'All right, all right!' I picked up the book for another look. 'I'm trying, but no one said I was going to have to do maths on a Saturday.'

Lucy went out into the hallway and shouted, 'Elllllllllllllla!' up the stairs.

Ella was definitely the right person to ask. She loves maths on a Saturday. She would probably even love maths on her birthday. She took one look at the recipe and told us that we needed to triple the recipe.

'Do you want me to write down the amounts?' she asked.

'No,' I said.

'Yes,' Lucy said.

So she wrote them down which did make things a bit easier.

Once we'd got the first batch of fairy cakes in the oven I gathered up everything we needed for the brownies. 'We'll do this while we're waiting,' I said. 'Thunder taught me how to make them. It's the easiest recipe in the world.'

Lucy twirled one of her apron strings. 'It would have to be easy for Thunder to be able to do it.'

I gave her a shove. 'For your information, Thunder is very good at cooking. He's going to be a chef when he grows up.'

Lucy didn't look convinced. 'Are you sure it's a proper recipe?'

'It's mostly chocolate spread. Everybody loves chocolate spread, don't they?'

She couldn't argue with that and we had the mixture done by the time the first lot of fairy cakes came out of the oven. We got the next batch in and then I suggested we watch TV while they were cooking.

'Shouldn't we wait here?' Lucy said.

'Nah, it's fine.'

So we went into the other room. And I really did remember about the cakes for the first few minutes, but then someone on TV was trying to break the world record for putting eggs into egg cups with their feet and it wasn't until I sniffed a nice cakey smell drifting into the room that I realised I'd totally forgotten about them.

'Oh no!' I leapt up and sprinted for the kitchen.

'They're ruined!' Lucy wailed when I pulled them out of the oven.

'They're not ruined.' Although some of them

did look rather black. 'Well, not all. The ones that were on the bottom shelf are perfect.'

'I wanted them all to be perfect!'

In the end we only had to throw away six burnt cakes. Then there were a few that were on the crunchy side that we decided to eat ourselves. Even so, we were still left with thirty-seven quite edible-looking cakes. Plus two trays of brownies and a Victoria sponge.

'That ought to be enough,' I said. 'Mum said some of the other teachers were bringing extra stuff to add.'

I made sure everything was switched off and then Lucy went to get changed for ballet. Mum was really pleased with what we'd made, although she did moan a bit when she started brushing Lucy's hair ready for ballet and found it had something sticky in it, but I pointed out that if you want your hair to really stay put in a bun, egg is way more effective than hairspray.

CHAPTER ✦ FOURTEEN

We chose Thunder's house to have an Adrenaline Club meeting on Monday because he lives roughly in the middle of everyone else's and there are always chocolate biscuits at his house.

'The first Adrenaline Club dare was awesome!' Thunder said as soon as everyone was sitting in his living room.

'Shhh!' I said. I could hear his mum out in the hallway and I didn't want any awkward questions about what we'd been up to.

'Oh right,' Thunder said. 'We're not allowed to talk about Adrenaline Club because it's a secret.'

'Don't be stupid,' Amirah said. 'We have to talk about it or we won't be able to plan any more dares, will we?'

'And talking about what we did is one of the best bits,' Riley said.

'Just don't talk about it in front of other people,' I said, pointing towards the hall.

Thunder nodded slowly.

We listened to Thunder's mum going upstairs and then Thunder said in a very loud whisper, 'Seriously, it was brilliant!'

I grinned. 'It was pretty good, wasn't it?'

Amirah curled her bottom lip. 'It was all right. But we didn't really do that much, did we?'

'Yeah we did,' Riley said. 'We crept into the Ghost School . . .'

'Not inside it,' Amirah interrupted. 'Just into the playground.'

'It's a haunted school,' I said. 'That means the playground too.'

'And we could have got caught,' Riley went on. 'And we went right up to the tree and Chloe touched the apple.'

Amirah was still pulling the sort of face that Amelia does when I offer her something that I've made in Food Tech.

'The point of Adrenaline Club,' I said, 'is to get your adrenaline flowing, make your heart beat fast.'

'My heart was going like crazy,' Thunder said.

'Mine too,' Riley agreed.

I remembered Amirah's face under that streetlight; I was absolutely sure that she'd been excited. 'You said it was good when we did it.'

She blinked. 'I said it wasn't bad.' Then, I think she properly remembered because she stopped being sniffy and relaxed her shoulders. 'I suppose it was kind of creepy. When we were running for the fence I sort of expected a bony hand on my shoulder.'

Thunder gave a delighted shiver. 'Ooooh!' He turned to me. 'So who's making up the next dare?'

'I am,' Amirah said.

For half a second I wondered if I should never have said that we'd take it in turns to make up dares so that I'd always be the one thinking of them but then I was quite excited to hear what Amirah had thought of.

'This time it's an individual dare,' Amirah said. 'That means we all have to do it, but one at a time.'

She paused. The tension was giving me butterflies. I think Thunder was holding his breath.

'Your challenge is to get into the head's office and to bring back a blue slip to prove you've been there.'

At our school if you're really naughty you get sent to Mrs Hamilton and she fills in a blue slip of paper saying exactly what horrible crime you've committed and then you have to take it home and get it signed. It's pretty clever really because having to go home and tell your parents about the stupid thing you've done is even worse than a detention. Although they give you a detention as well, just in case having the headteacher, your mum, and your dad shout at you wasn't enough.

Thunder whistled.

'That's impossible!' Riley said. 'Mrs Hamilton is always in her office. And if she did go out for a bit you'd have to go past her secretary and the secretary would see you. There's no way anyone could do that without getting caught.'

It was definitely high risk. You'd have to be pretty crazy to try it. 'I could do it,' I said.

Amirah grinned at me. 'I knew you'd be up for something really tricky.'

'It's not just tricky.' Thunder shook his head. 'Even if you managed to find a time when she and her secretary weren't there, you wouldn't know when they were coming back. They could walk right in and catch you. It would be terrifying.' He pulled at his jumper. 'It's making me sweat just thinking about it.'

I winked at him. 'That's why we call it Adrenaline Club.'

CHAPTER ✱ FIFTEEN

My dad lent me the biography of a spy once. I thought it was going to be really exciting. Some of it was, but there were long stretches of boring bits because apparently being a spy is like that. You have to do a lot of planning and then finally you go off on a mission and that's when things get dangerous. When I gave it back to my dad, I told him that I'd learnt that being a spy isn't just about sneaking around places and shooting people, you actually have to do a lot of preparation. He said that maybe I should take the same approach with my homework. I pointed out that if you're a spy and you don't prepare, you might end up with someone using a razor-sharp bowler hat to Frisbee your head off, whereas even though detention is super boring, it's never actually killed anyone.

But thinking about the spy book, I decided it was probably worth doing some planning for the new Adrenaline Club challenge. The most important thing was to work out when Mrs Hamilton and her secretary were most likely to be out of their offices at the same time. I thought about all the reasons why Mrs Hamilton might leave her office: teaching a lesson, going to the loo, getting something to eat, taking someone on a tour around the school. I didn't think her secretary would be going with her for any of that. I spent two whole days thinking about it, but I couldn't seem to come up with any solutions. In the end I decided that I needed to take this problem to the smartest person I know.

Ella was lying on her bed in our bedroom at Dad's house reading a book.

'I've got a problem,' I said, sitting down on the floor. 'I need two things to happen at the same time so that something else can happen. But I don't think that the two things will ever happen at the same time.'

The great thing about Ella is that if you ask her a question she does her best to answer it without getting nosy about what exactly you're talking about.

She thought for a moment and then she said, 'If it's impossible or almost impossible to achieve those conditions in order to reach your desired outcome then it may be best to consider whether there is actually a different set of conditions that could lead to the same outcome.'

'What?'

I had to get her to explain it again, and then again in different words and in the end I got it. Basically, she was saying that if the head and her secretary weren't going to clear off at the same time, then could I think of a way to get into the head's office without that happening? I didn't see how, because the secretary's desk was right by the door to the head's office and how else was I going to get in except through the door ... unless, of course, I went in by the window.

'Yes!' I said out loud.

Ella's eyebrows went up. 'Has that helped?' she asked.

'I think you might have solved my problem.'

'Good.' She smiled. And even then she didn't ask me what the heck I was going on about.

I hugged Ella. 'Thanks.'

I went downstairs to the kitchen. Amelia was playing on her phone and Suvi was on the other side of the room looking at some work papers.

'Ella's brilliant,' I said to Amelia.

'What's brilliant?' she asked, looking up from

her phone. 'Never mind, I already know what's brilliant. It's absolutely nothing. Everything is terrible.'

She looked miserable. She'd been worrying about Lauren. 'Is Lauren still off school?' I asked.

Amelia's shoulders sagged. 'Yeah. It seems like she's getting really bad again. And she won't be able to come to Community Choir on Sunday.'

'That's rough,' I said. 'But they said it was okay, didn't they? If she missed it sometimes?'

'Mm, but it's not the same without her. I might give it a miss too.'

I was surprised by that, because even though Amelia is lazy about homework and putting her cereal bowl in the sink, she is always really strict about anything to do with singing. She's never missed a school rehearsal for anything.

'I thought you loved it there.'

Amelia shrugged. 'I do like it. We have a laugh, but sometimes I wish that people would concentrate a bit more on their singing. Our teacher knows what she's talking about but people don't always listen and they make mistakes.'

I couldn't see what the big deal was. 'Everybody makes mistakes. Even Amelia the Greatest makes mistakes. You're always going on about the things that you need to improve.'

'That's the point,' she said. 'I try to learn from my mistakes and avoid doing them again but sometimes I think there are people in our choir who don't even really care about getting it right.'

I don't know how Amelia can be bothered to be so bothered about what other people are doing all the time. 'Does it matter if they're getting it wrong?' I asked. 'As long as you're doing it right?'

Amelia pursed her lips. 'Of course it matters. It makes us sound amateurish.'

I wasn't completely sure what amateurish meant but I could tell that Amelia thought it was something awful.

'Also, I'm not sure that they really realise what Lauren and I can do.'

I could hardly believe that. Amelia never misses a chance to do her warbly singing in people's faces. 'Why do you think that?'

'Last week we were doing a song with a solo and instead of choosing the person who would be best suited to it . . .'

I knew that meant choosing Amelia.

'. . . or even trying a few people out, Merinda just let any old one volunteer.'

She was getting really worked up.

'I feel completely underappreciated. They don't seem to realise that I'm talented.'

'I know how that feels. It's like being the best rugby player and not even getting chosen to go to training camp.'

Amelia squinted. She obviously hadn't thought about things being similar for us two.

'*Ohhh*,' she said. 'Yeah. It is like that. I'm really good at singing and you're really good at ... throwing balls, and we're not being valued.'

I realised that Suvi had stopped looking at her report and was listening to everything we were saying.

'Don't you think?' I asked her. 'That people aren't being very fair on us?'

Suvi pushed her papers to one side. 'I'm thinking that maybe you two do not value your coaches.'

Amelia stiffened.

'I do value Coach,' I said. 'He's a brilliant player and he's taught me some cool stuff. I think he's awesome.'

'But not enough to trust his judgement?'

I folded my arms on the table. 'Not if he's going to make stupid judgements. Everyone knows I'm the best so I should be going to that camp. It's simple.'

'You're the best?'

'Yes! You've seen me play rugby.'

'She is good,' Amelia said. 'The PE teachers say so.'

'I think this is not just about how good you are at running and tackling.'

Amelia rolled her eyes. 'What else would it be about?'

'Are you the best at taking instruction? Are you the best at keeping your temper if your team loses? Are you the best at getting better?'

She was starting to sound like Coach. Maybe I'm not the best at those things but it was making me feel all hot just hearing her say that stuff. I didn't want to think about it. 'Why are grown-ups always trying to make out that playing nicely is more important than playing well?' I said. Even though I knew that wasn't exactly what she meant. 'They're just trying to trick you into being good. Your behaviour isn't the point in rugby.'

Suvi looked me right in the eye. 'I think it is. I think it is the point that your coach is trying to make by not picking you for the camp. If you want to be a really good player then it is about the way you behave, and the way that you think, as well as how you play. In fact, those things will make you play better if you have the right attitude.'

I sort of knew she was right. 'I suppose so.' Top sports people do always talk about how important

105

mental attitude is. But I still thought that Coach was mostly punishing me for missing a few lousy training sessions.

'What about me?' Amelia asked. 'No one can say I'm not dedicated; I always go to choir, even when Lauren can't, and I definitely work the hardest out of anyone there.'

'Is that what your coach wants from you? You joined this choir because they are relaxed and kind and they do not mind if poor Lauren cannot attend. But now you criticise their relaxed attitude and their inclusive approach. You can't have all things.'

Amelia's face was like stone, but I was pretty sure that underneath her frozen features she was furious. I didn't feel too happy myself. Deep down I knew that what Suvi was saying made sense but I was still too hurt and cross to want to really admit it. I wasn't ready to forgive Coach yet and even though I was missing rugby so much, I wasn't ready to be sorry.

CHAPTER 🍓 SIXTEEN

Since we'd made the cakes together, Lucy seemed pretty busy; she was either out in the garden talking to Mrs Partridge or holed up in the Pit writing in one of her evil plans books. The books are exercise books that she gets Mum to bring home from work for her. Lucy doesn't write *evil plans* on the front, or anything like that, but we all know that any time she's scribbling away in one that she's writing down schemes for something terrible.

After tea on Thursday, Amelia and I found Lucy curled up on the sofa in the Pit when we went down there to look for the TV remote, which had completely disappeared. One of her evil plans books was on her lap and she was chewing her pencil.

'What are you writing?' I asked.

Lucy snapped the book shut, but not before I saw that she'd written DOG WALKS in large letters. 'Dog walks? What's that supposed to mean?'

She crossed her eyes. 'Dog walks, you know, walks for dogs. I'm going to get people to pay me to take their dogs for walks.'

I felt behind the cushions for the remote. 'When you put it in capitals like that it sounds like a headline in a newspaper. Like they're reporting on this amazing dog that can walk.'

'All dogs can walk,' Amelia said.

'I mean on its back legs like a human.' I got down on my hands and knees to look under the sofa. 'Or it could be about a very sick dog that got told it would never walk again and then it did. Wow! DOG WALKS!'

'How would it know that it was never going to walk again?' Lucy asked. 'It wouldn't have understood when they told it, would it? It would have just carried on thinking one day it would get better and walk again.'

I sat back on my heels. 'That's probably a good way to deal with not being able to walk.'

Amelia was staring at us. 'When you two have finished with your dog philosophy and are ready to get back to what was actually being talked about,

I've got a few sane-person questions to ask about Lucy's crazy plan.'

Lucy's eyes turned to slits and bore into Amelia.

'Ahem,' Amelia coughed. 'I mean Lucy's latest bold venture.'

'What's a bold venture?' Lucy asked me.

'It's a good thing,' I said. 'You don't need to laser-eye her again.'

Lucy opened her book again and started drawing. It looked like she was making a poster for her new idea. 'What's your question, Amelia?'

'How are you going to take dogs for a walk when you're not even allowed out of the house on your own?'

Last year, Lucy had this crazy idea that Dad and Suvi and Kirsti should come and live with us, so she basically kidnapped Kirsti, which made everybody freak out and then Lucy had to promise never to go anywhere without a big sister or a grown-up.

Lucy rolled her eyes. 'Obviously someone will have to come with me.'

'I did the cakes,' I said, as fast as I could, just in case anyone thought I ought to be volunteering.

'What's in it for the person who goes with you?' Amelia looked down at the poster. I think the picture was supposed to be Lucy taking a dog for a walk but it looked more like she was strangling him with a piece of rope. 'Are you going to share your fee with them?'

'No,' Lucy said. 'I can't do that because I wouldn't have as much money.'

Amelia folded her arms. 'So ... for absolutely no reward you want me to drag myself to the park with a flea-bitten mongrel.' She paused. 'And a dog.'

I couldn't help laughing, even though we're not supposed to encourage Amelia when she's being rude because sometimes when she gets started she doesn't know how to stop.

'Why on earth would I do that?' Amelia asked.

Lucy shook back her shiny curls and put on her Christmas-angel face. She smiled up at Amelia and batted her eyelashes. 'Because you love your ickle sister?' She sounded like one of those advert children who talk like toddlers.

I passed Amelia a cowboy hat from the dressing-up box and she pretended to be sick in it. 'I will absolutely never ever take you anywhere with any animal if you ever say "ickle" again.'

Lucy snapped her eyes down, immediately business-like again. 'Fine,' she said. She flipped to another page in her book with dates written on it. 'I'll put you on all the days from Monday to Friday. Chloe can do Saturday and Sunday.'

'Hang on!' I said. 'I didn't say I'd do that.'

Amelia rummaged through one of the toy boxes, still looking for the remote. 'Don't worry about it, Clo, I bet my life she hasn't cleared this with Mum, have you, Lucy?'

'Not yet,' Lucy said. She obviously didn't think it would be a problem. 'Don't worry about Mum. I can take care of her.'

Amelia shook her head like the whole thing was crazy, but we hadn't completely wasted our time because I found the remote sticking out of a princess shoe in the dressing-up box.

CHAPTER ✦ SEVENTEEN

It turned out that we didn't have to fight about who was going to help Lucy walk dogs because Amelia was right; when Lucy told Mum about it at breakfast the next day, it was definitely one of those brilliant ideas that Mum didn't think was brilliant, and this time there was no school dog-walking that Mum could offer as a second choice.

'You can't go round knocking on doors begging for money,' she said.

Lucy looked insulted. 'I wasn't going to beg. They were going to pay me for doing a job.'

'You're not knocking on doors. You never know who might answer.'

'I wasn't going to knock, that would take ages. I was going to put up a poster with our telephone number and address on.'

Mum tutted. 'And what have I said about never giving those details out?'

'But I'm not giving them to a dangerous person, I'm just sticking them on a lamp post.'

'Murderers walk past lamp posts too,' Amelia pointed out from behind her book.

Mum started stacking cereal bowls. 'Sorry, Lucy, but this scheme isn't happening.'

Lucy pouted. 'Don't you want me to make any money?'

'It's not high on my list. I'd rather that you did your reading for school and put your dirty washing in the basket.' And she went into the sitting room to hunt for Lucy's book bag.

Lucy looked furious. Ella looked worried. She doesn't like other people to be unhappy.

'Maybe you could do something else for Mrs Partridge,' Ella suggested. 'You could make her a card.'

Lucy snorted. 'She's not one of those soppy ladies like Granny who think the best thing is a stupid drawing a little kid does! She thinks the best gift is cold, hard cash. She told me.'

'You'll have to think of another way to make money then,' I said.

'I've tried! Mum only let me do cakes once. I told people at school I could cut their hair and do make-overs but no one wants me too. I asked in two shops if they could let me work but they just laughed.'

This was news to me. And I was pretty certain that Lucy hadn't even been in any shops by herself.

'When did you do that?' I asked.

'When Mum was looking at something.'

She's pretty sneaky. I was sort of impressed, but Lucy wasn't noticing me being impressed; she was busy working herself into what Mum calls 'a state'.

'Now I can't walk dogs,' she whined. 'There isn't anything else I can *dooooooooooo* to make *moneeeeeeeeey*,' she wailed, and flopped face down on the table.

Amelia looked up from her book. 'Yes, there is,' she said. 'You can be my tweenie.'

Lucy's head jerked back up. I waited for her to tell Amelia that there was no way she was going to be her maid. But she didn't. Instead she said, 'Really? You'll pay me?'

Amelia blinked a bit; I don't think that was the reaction she was expecting from Lucy. 'Yes, I mean . . .'

'Fifty pee? Every day that I do it? I can't do it when I'm at school but I can when I come home.'

Amelia looked a bit shifty. 'Um, okay.'

'Oh, thank you, Amelia.' And she sprung out of her chair and flung her arms around her.

Then Mum came back and started telling Lucy that she needed to put her shoes on and after she'd said it about fifty-seven times, Lucy did put her shoes on and Mum said goodbye and drove Lucy off to Breakfast Club.

Ella went upstairs to brush her hair. I looked at the clock. There was just time for one more thing to eat. I grabbed a bowl from the fridge and sat back down.

Amelia peered over the top of her book. 'I can't believe you're eating cold spaghetti bolognese for breakfast.'

I shrugged; there isn't a time of day when I wouldn't eat spaghetti bolognese. 'I can't believe you tricked Lucy into being your tweenie.'

Amelia looked sheepish. 'Neither can I.' She marked her place in her book with a teaspoon. 'And I didn't trick her.'

'I s'pose not. I just can't believe she agreed to it. She hated picking up your stuff when we played it when we were little.'

'I know. I feel a bit bad.'

'What do you mean?'

'When I suggested it, it just slipped out of my mouth. I think I sort of did it to wind her up.

And . . .' She gave an uncomfortable wriggle. 'I shouldn't wind her up.'

'Why not? You love winding people up.'

'Yeah, but recently I've realised that sometimes it's okay to mess with you lot and sometimes it's not.'

Amelia can be quite a difficult person to live with. When our parents split up it made her really sad and angry and she took some of that anger out on us, her sisters. Since she had a big heart-to-heart with my dad she's been more like the old Amelia. Recently, even though she still loves taking the mickey, it's seemed like she's tried particularly hard not to say anything really awful, but I didn't realise that she was following some kind of rules. 'What do you mean?' I asked.

'When Lucy is being revolting, I think it's all right to make fun of her, but she's totally serious about making money for this old lady and when you think about that, it's actually kind of sweet.'

I spat a little bit of bolognese out. A few flecks went on Amelia's school jumper.

'Chloe!' She rubbed at her front with a tea towel.

'Sorry, sorry, I just don't think I've heard you call Lucy sweet before.' I hesitated. 'I don't think I've ever heard anyone call her sweet.'

'You know what I'm saying. I don't want to be nasty about this.'

I knew what she meant. When we used to play Tweenies, Amelia was always the one who thought up really horrible jobs for whoever was being the maid.

'You're not really doing anything nasty, yet,' I said. 'It will only be nasty when you start making her rub your feet and fetch you biscuits in the middle of the night.'

Amelia twisted her mouth. 'Maybe I won't do that.'

I swallowed my last mouthful of spaghetti. 'You won't?'

'She could just be my tweenie for two days a week.'

That did not sound like Amelia.

'On my washing-up nights.'

That sounded more like Amelia.

She stood up and crammed her book into her school bag. 'I mean, she ought to do something for her money. She can do my washing-up and maybe help me when I cook tea and that way I'll be helping her make money without taking advantage.'

'That seems . . . fair,' I said.

She screwed up her face. 'Ugh, it really does,

doesn't it?' She shooed me out of the kitchen and into the hall to pick up my bag. 'We'd better get to school quickly in case I have to do something terrible in a minute just to make up for it.'

CHAPTER ❤ EIGHTEEN

When I got to school, I decided to do a quick bit of what spies call *reconnaissance*. That means checking out the area where you're hoping to carry out a mission. It turned out that the window of Mrs Hamilton's office is in a really good position for someone who wants to sneak inside. Firstly, because it's round the side of the school where pupils aren't supposed to go, there would be no one about to see me climbing in. Secondly, it's screened from the main road by bushes, so people driving past wouldn't spot me and think I was a burglar or anything silly. Best of all, the sun was shining and the window was already open a crack. All I had to do was hope it wouldn't start raining before the afternoon.

By asking around, I'd found out that Mrs

Hamilton teaches a couple of lessons and one is on a Friday afternoon. I figured that the safest time for sneaking into her office was definitely while she was taking a class so all I had to do was get myself out of my own lesson for long enough to nab the blue slip. So I turned up for geography as usual, then I waited till Miss Dalgleish had finished her opening ramble and then put up my hand.

'I've left my pen in the library. Please can I go and get it?'

Miss Dalgleish sighed. 'You'll have to get it at the end of school. You can borrow one of mine for now.'

That wasn't what she was supposed to say.

'But it was expensive,' I said. 'My dad gave it to me.' All of which was completely true. 'If it gets left in the library someone might nick it.'

'Yeah,' said Melanie Styles, joining in. '8PW have got library time now and everyone knows that that lot are always pinching stuff.'

'No, they're not!' someone else called out.

'Oh yeah?' Melanie asked. 'What about that time I left my phone in their tutor room an—'

'All right, all right!' Miss Dalgleish said. 'Chloe, you may fetch your pen. I expect you back here in less than five minutes.'

I pushed back my chair and grinned at her.

The library is a bit closer to our geography room than Mrs Hamilton's office so I knew I had to be speedy. I trotted through the corridors as fast as I thought I could go without drawing attention to myself.

When I got outside I kept myself flat against the wall as I approached the head's office; I needed to check that Mrs Hamilton really was out of the room. I crept closer until I could see inside.

Empty.

Good. I crouched low and shuffled along until I was directly under the window, which was still ajar. I stuck my hand up to pull it further open. It was a bit stiff and the way it was attached to the frame meant that it only opened so far. I eyed the gap; it was just about big enough for me to get through, but I hoped I wouldn't need to get out again in a hurry.

Slowly, I stood up. Everything was quiet. I took a quick look over my shoulder then I lifted one leg up and over so I was straddling the windowsill. I had to wriggle a bit to get through. The minute my feet touched the ground it occurred to me that just because Mrs Hamilton was busy in her lesson, it didn't mean that no one would come in. Maybe her secretary would want to put some letters on her desk, or a kid might get sent to see her. The thought of the door opening was so horrible that for a moment I was paralysed. But I knew that I had to move fast. I took a lunging step towards the desk and grabbed the top blue slip from the pile and stuffed it into my pocket, then I turned to move back towards the window.

And that's when I heard the door open behind me.

A voice said, 'What are you doing in here?'

A hot, sick feeling washed right over me. I turned round, expecting to see the secretary, or a teacher, or even Mrs Hamilton herself, despite the fact I knew it wasn't her voice.

It wasn't any of those people. It was a prefect. The one that is sometimes on late duty by the student entrance.

'Mrs Hamilton told me to wait here for her,' I said.

I don't know where that came from. It just popped right out of my mouth and it was probably the best thing that I could have said because she just said, 'Oh.' And she hung the clipboard she was holding on a hook on the wall and walked right back out again.

My legs were shaking so much that I could hardly clamber back out of the window but I did it pretty quickly and then I ran all the way back to my geography classroom.

'Are you feeling all right?' Miss Dalgleish asked, when I was back in my seat. 'You look a bit flushed.'

'You said five minutes. I didn't want to miss anything.' I was trying not to pant. 'I'm completely fine.'

But actually my heart was zooming and my fingertips were prickling. I didn't feel fine at all.

I felt amazing.

CHAPTER ♥ NINETEEN

We were all sitting around reading on Sunday morning at Dad's house when we heard him talking on the phone in the hall. We have to read a lot at Dad's house because there's no TV. Actually, I was spotting Wally in one of Thunder's *Where's Wally?* books, but that's probably better for you than reading because being able to spot stuff is a really useful skill. I wasn't especially listening to what Dad was saying, but I did hear him say, 'Or you could tell her when she gets home?' My ears pricked up a bit at that because whenever my dad says 'her' or 'she' it means he's talking about one of us. Next he said, 'No, you're right. It's best I break it to her now.'

I couldn't concentrate on Wally then because I was trying to work out what might be going on.

A few minutes later Dad came in and I wondered who was getting the bad news.

'Lucy, can I talk to you?' Dad asked.

Uh-oh. When Lucy gets told things she doesn't want to hear it's usually very loud.

Lucy looked at him suspiciously. 'Is it about that bruise that Isla Heartford has got? Because I don't know how it got there and it wasn't because I pushed her in the playground even if she says it was.'

'It's not about that.' Dad sat down and patted the sofa next to him. 'Why don't you come and sit here for a minute?'

Lucy got up and sat next to him. Ella shot me a look. Lucy didn't know it but we could feel something really bad was going to happen.

Dad put an arm around Lucy.

'You know that Mrs Partridge has been poorly, don't you?'

Lucy nodded. 'She said she wasn't, but she didn't want any of my chocolate fingers and they're her favourites.'

'In fact, she's so poorly that she's had to go into hospital.'

'Oh,' Lucy said. 'Is that why she didn't even come and say something rude to me when I shouted through her letterbox yesterday?'

Dad's face went through several different expressions till he said, 'I expect so. But what I want you to understand is that she's very ill and she's also very old.' He took a deep breath. 'I'm sorry to have to tell you this, sweetheart, but she's going to die.'

'Everybody dies, dummy.'

'Yes, but I'm afraid that the doctors think that Mrs Partridge is going to die very soon.'

Lucy stared at him. She stared so long and so hard that I started to wonder if she had heard. Dad gave her a sort of sympathetic almost-smile and reached for her hand.

Lucy snatched her hand away. 'That is the stupidest thing I've ever heard!' she spat. Then she wriggled from under his arm and walked out of the room. We heard her clomping up the stairs to our bedroom.

'Poor Lucy,' Ella said. 'I think this is going to be very difficult for her.'

A door upstairs slammed.

'I think it's going to be difficult for all of us,' Amelia said.

*

Lucy stayed upstairs for hours. She didn't come down until after we'd had lunch and Amelia had left to go to Community Choir. For a while she just sat in a chair scowling but then Ella asked her to play cards with me and her, and she agreed.

After a few games we heard singing out in the hall and we knew Amelia was back. She slammed open the sitting-room door and burst in with a flying leap.

'*Laaaaaaaa!*' she sang.

Community Choir always made her a bit crazy.

'*La la la la laaaaaaaa!* I'm going to be famous.'

Lucy looked up and I wondered if she was about to start a fight.

'Is this famous like when Chloe set off those stink bombs in the French room and got told off in front of the whole school?' she asked.

'That's not famous, that's just embarrassing.' Ella looked green at the thought of being hauled up in front of everybody.

I didn't think they were being very fair to me. 'You say it's not famous, but actually quite a few people asked me for my autograph.'

Amelia clapped her hands. 'Back to me. There's a proper professional touring company doing a musical of *Little Women* at the Corn Exchange.

127

They want to choose a local girl to be Amy at the beginning of the show.'

'The beginning?' Ella asked. 'But isn't she one of the main parts?'

Amelia took a breath like she was being very patient and we were all being a bit slow. 'Yes, but at the start of the book she's young and then later on she grows up, doesn't she? They want someone to play her when she's little.'

'You're not little,' Lucy said.

Amelia narrowed her eyes. 'I could look little. She's twelve or something at the beginning. I've only just stopped being thirteen.'

Ella and I exchanged looks. Most of the time Amelia refers to herself as *fourteen and a half*.

Amelia stood in front of the mirror and smoothed her fringe. 'I found out about it at Community Choir. Merinda is friends with one of the producers.'

I gave her a poke. 'I thought you said Merinda was an old hippy.'

'She is. She's an old hippy who knows some really cool people.'

'Does that mean she'll get you an audition?' Ella asked.

Amelia tutted. 'They're letting any-old-body audition. They're going to put it in the paper and everything. But Merinda is going to recommend me; that's what's going to make me stand out. That, and my beautiful singing voice.'

'Don't forget your modesty and humble attitude,' I said.

Amelia gave me an annoying smile. 'You've got to be confident in your abilities if you want to succeed.'

Actually, she was right about that. If you're good at something, I think you should be able to say it. I hate it when people pretend to think they're rubbish at things and say, *Oh, look at my stupid drawing,* so that you'll tell them it's good. 'Fair enough,' I said. 'I'm just making sure that you're tough enough to take some teasing.'

'I'm tough enough.' Then her face fell. 'I wish Lauren could audition too.'

Ella's face clouded with sympathy. 'Did her mum say no?'

'She doesn't need to. We all know that Lauren's too sick. She's still having a bad patch.' She sat down heavily in the armchair.

'Do you want to talk about it?' Ella asked.

Amelia shook her head. I was worried she might cry. I shot the other two a panicked look. Lucy wasn't paying any attention; she was busy trying to balance a two-pence piece on her forehead. But I could see that Ella understood. We needed to distract Amelia. The best way I could think of was to get her talking, and the thing Amelia loves talking about most is herself so I said, 'Right . . . tell us about this *Little People* part, then.'

Amelia rubbed her face. 'Little *Women*. Did I tell you it's going to be in the Corn Exchange? It will be my first time in a proper theatre and there'll be hundreds of people in the audience. I get to wear an old-fashioned dress and have my hair done, maybe in ringlets or something and I'll be on right at the beginning and I get to sing with the other sisters for two songs.'

She was making it sound like she'd already got the part, but at least she seemed a bit happier.

'Is that all?' Lucy asked. 'If I was going to be in a musical then I'd be singing all the songs.'

Amelia wrinkled her nose. 'You wouldn't be in a musical.'

'No, I wouldn't because I don't want to. But if I want to do something then I absolutely always can do it.'

Nobody wanted to say anything about that because we were all trying not to upset her after what Dad had told her about Mrs Partridge. But in a slightly scary way I thought it was probably true.

I have never met anyone as determined as Lucy. I bet Lucy would have found a way of getting to the rugby camp.

I just hoped Amelia wasn't going to be disappointed if it turned out she didn't have Lucy's sticking power.

CHAPTER ✿ TWENTY

During registration on Monday morning I decided it was time to enjoy sharing my success with the rest of Adrenaline Club so I nudged Thunder and then pulled the corner of the blue slip I'd nabbed from Mrs Hamilton's office out of my pocket. His mouth fell open.

'You didn't!' he whispered, while Mrs Montgomery was calling out the register.

I smiled mysteriously.

Being mysterious is quite fun but not as good as telling the whole story, so by the time we walked into the chemistry lab I'd told him everything. His eyes got wider and wider as I went on.

'Aren't you worried?' he asked when I'd finished.

I steered him into a seat near the back. 'What about?'

'That prefect. What if she tells Mrs Hamilton you were there?'

'Why would she do that? She probably thinks I was there to be told off. She's not going to run up to the head and say, "How did it go with that naughty Year Eight?", is she?'

Thunder rummaged in his bag for his book. 'So you're not worried?'

I shrugged. 'I bet she's forgotten all about it already.'

'She might see you around school and it might jog her memory.'

I pulled a strand of hair across my top lip. 'I'd better start wearing a fake moustache then.'

But he didn't laugh, in fact, he had a face like someone had died. He actually seemed quite bothered about me being caught out. I suppose it was sort of sweet that he was worrying about me getting into trouble.

'Listen, Thunder, it's not like I did anything really wrong. I didn't break anything or make a mess. It's not hurting anyone, is it?'

'I s'pose.'

I had a look in his pencil case for a pen to borrow. 'So, when are you going to get your blue slip?'

'Me?' He sounded so surprised that you'd have thought I'd never mentioned it before.

'I dunno. After what happened to you I'm not sure about it.'

'Chicken,' I said.

'I'm not chicken it's just … well, you've done it now.'

'We said we'd all do it. I bet Amirah does it.'

'I know …' He wriggled uncomfortably.

Mr Chadwick came out of the prep room and into the lab and I knew I only had a few seconds to say something to convince Thunder to do the dare. Sometimes Thunder is a bit down on himself and I knew if he managed to do this it would give him a real boost. Besides, I didn't want Amirah saying he ought to be out of the club if he couldn't do the dares.

'Amirah's pretty cool, isn't she?' I said. 'Really brave. She's exactly what a member of the Adrenaline Club should be.'

And I had to leave it at that because Mr Chadwick was giving me the stink eye.

When school finished I bumped into Ella on the stairs.

'Hellooooo!' I said, lifting my hand to give her a high five. Thunder had finally agreed that he was going to give the dare a go and I was feeling pretty good.

'Um, hello,' Ella said, giving me a very gentle five. It was more of pat.

We carried on down the stairs to go and meet Amelia to walk home.

'Hey, Ella!' someone shouted.

We both turned round to see who was calling her. It was Carys, our head girl, and she was striding towards us. I looked at Ella. She seemed so panicked that for a second I wondered if she was in trouble, before I remembered that this was Ella. I suddenly thought of the prefect who'd seen me in the head's office, but when Carys caught up with us, she was only interested in Ella.

'That was a good meeting at lunchtime,' she said. 'Thanks for volunteering to do that research. I just wanted to let you know that I've been talking to Mrs Hamilton and she's agreed that we can present our idea about student mentors to the school at the next whole-school assembly.'

'Oh,' Ella said.

'I know, great news, hey? I was thinking that you could talk about the findings of your research, but we can sort out exactly who's going to say what at the next meeting. Okay?'

Ella didn't say anything. But Carys isn't the kind of girl to wait around for an answer or even to notice that not everybody is the same super-confident loud type that she is, so she turned away and called, 'See you next week!' over her shoulder.

I was watching Ella. She looked like our pet rabbit, Buttercup, does when Lucy tries to persuade her to do a magic trick.

'You don't want to speak in assembly, do you?' I said.

She shook her head.

'If you don't want to do it, then you just have to tell them.'

Ella opened her mouth but nothing came out. She was never going to say 'no' to the head girl.

'Don't worry,' I said. 'It's just an assembly. You probably won't have to say much.'

That horrible crease that Ella sometimes gets between her eyes appeared. I really wanted to call Carys back and tell her that Ella wouldn't be speaking in her stupid assembly but I knew Ella would never forgive me.

I put my arm around her. 'It will be all right,' I said.

We both knew that was a big fat lie, but I really wanted to make things better for her and that was the only thing I had to say.

CHAPTER ❤ TWENTY-ONE

I was starting my third sandwich on Friday lunchtime when Riley came rushing up to me.

'Something's happened,' he said.

I wiped some mayonnaise off my chin. 'What?'

'It's Thunder,' he said, clutching my arm. 'He's in the exclusion room.'

I was a bit annoyed because that meant he wouldn't be in geography next lesson and I'd have to sit by myself. 'That's not big news,' I said. 'He's been there before. Remember when he tried to light his fart with a Bunsen burner?'

'You don't understand.' He looked over his shoulder and then lowered his voice. 'It was the dare, he was going sneak into the . . .' He mouthed the words *head's office* as if saying it out loud would set off an alarm.

I shook his hand off my arm. 'Are you sure?' It was one thing for Thunder to get himself into trouble; it was a bit different if he'd wound up in the exclusion room because of Adrenaline Club.

Riley sat down. 'He definitely said he was going to do it. He said he didn't want to get kicked out of the club so he had to do it.' He bit his lip. 'That was the last thing he said to me.'

'He's not died, you idiot!' I screwed up my sandwich bag. I couldn't believe Thunder had mucked it up. I should have given him some help. 'There's no point getting worked up about it. Fridays are busy in the exclusion room. Maybe they won't have time to phone his mum.' I squashed down thoughts about what Thunder's mum might say to him. It was too late to help him now. I took a bite of my apple and tried to think about something else. 'Have you done your biology homework?'

Riley stared at me. 'Don't you care?'

I was starting to feel a bit uncomfortable. *Of course* I felt bad about Thunder but I didn't like the way Riley was staring at me. 'About Thunder?' I shrugged. 'He's a bit of a turnip but I'll forgive him.'

'But he's in big trouble and it's our fault.'

I really didn't want that to be true so I said, 'It's

not our fault,' much more firmly than I believed it. 'We didn't go stomping into the office at the wrong time.'

'It's your club's dare.'

I was starting to get annoyed now. I felt all guilty and horrible inside and I just wanted Riley to stop going on about it. 'It was Amirah's dare and it's Thunder's mess up. You have to take responsibility for your own mistakes. My dad's always telling me that.'

Riley still looked like Ella does when she's trodden on a worm. 'What if he talks about you-know-what? What if he tells them everything and we all get called to see the head?'

Even though I didn't quite know if this was my fault or not, there was one thing that I was absolutely sure about and that was that Thunder is my best friend and that he is the most loyal person in the world.

'Thunder won't tell,' I said.

Geography was pretty boring with no one to talk to. RE was a bit better because we sit around tables of eight so I had other people to chat with. But even while I was joking about, I couldn't stop thinking about Thunder. How much trouble was he in?

At the end of the day, I waited for Thunder outside the exclusion room. He looked exhausted when he came through the door.

'What happened?' I asked. 'Did you get caught in the head's office?'

He nodded. 'Don't make me talk about it now. I'm worn out.'

'All right. How was the exclusion room? Did you have a nice time with the naughty kids?'

Thunder sagged into a massive sigh. 'Man, it is so quiet in there that I sometimes wish my head would explode just so there can be a noise. You have to sit there in total, total silence and only look at your work. We were doing that for about a million years and it was so still that I was just going to fall asleep and then Sahil did an enormous burp and everyone started cracking up and Miss Reece went mad at us.' He gave me a big grin but then his face froze. 'I've got to go home and tell my mum.'

'Will she be cross?'

'Yeah.'

'What are you going to say?'

Thunder pressed his lips together in thought. 'Dunno. I'd better go and get it over with.' He sighed again. 'See you tomorrow. If my mum hasn't flattened me.'

She probably could, as well. The only person

I know who is taller and wider than Thunder is Thunder's mum. 'Good luck,' I called after him.

'What does he need good luck for?' Amirah asked, coming up behind me.

'He got caught sneaking into the head's office.'

Amirah whistled. 'That's bad.' She shook her head. 'He's not really cut out for this sort of thing. You shouldn't have made him do it.'

In my heart, I already knew that, but everybody blaming it all on me was just making me feel like screaming. 'I didn't make him! It was your dare. It was his choice.'

'He wanted to impress you.'

'Don't be stupid.' It was like they'd all forgotten about Adrenaline Club. 'He was just doing the dare; that's what the club is about. If he doesn't like it, or he can't do it without getting caught, then he doesn't have to be a member, does he?' I felt bad the minute the words were out of my mouth. The whole reason I talked Thunder into doing the dare was because I didn't want anyone to say he should be kicked out. If Thunder ever left the club so would I.

Amirah looked at me like I was getting worked up over nothing. 'I'm just saying that Thunder and Riley think you're great, and they'll basically do anything you say, so maybe you should be careful about what you encourage them to do. We both should be careful.'

I shrugged, which I think she might have thought was a 'yes' because she gave me a thumbs-up and strolled off.

I thought about what she'd said while I was walking home with Ella and Amelia. I did feel sorry for Thunder getting into trouble, but Amirah was talking nonsense. Did she think we should choose a nice gentle dare like skipping through the corridor? This was supposed to be Adrenaline Club, not Everybody-Have-A-Nice-Relaxing-Day Club. Thunder is pretty good at bouncing back. He'd get over this and I could stop feeling bad and we could all go back to having an exciting time doing proper dares.

CHAPTER ♥ TWENTY–TWO

On Saturday morning, I got a lift to the park with Mum and Lucy on their way to Lucy's ballet lesson.

Riley and Amirah were already there but we had to wait ages for Thunder.

'I thought you'd be grounded,' Amirah said to him, when he finally turned up.

'Nah, my mum doesn't like me cluttering up the house. She's taken away my phone and my laptop instead.'

'Tough,' Riley said.

'Never mind that, the first thing we need to discuss is what on earth happened to you yesterday,' I said to Thunder.

'Did you just walk in on the head?' Riley asked.

Thunder plopped himself down beside me on the grass. 'No! I didn't try and go in until she was out. I'm not an idiot, am I?'

Amirah didn't look too sure about that.

'I hung about in the corridor and she went marching off somewhere with the caretaker so I thought that was my chance.'

'What about her secretary?' I asked.

Thunder rubbed his chin. 'I had a plan for her; I told her some boys were writing rude stuff on the wall outside Miss Dalgleish's room.'

That wasn't a bad idea.

'So she gets up and goes out and I slipped in, but then all of a sudden she's back again and saying *what are you doing in there?* and looking at me like I'm a burglar.'

Amirah shook her head at his stupidity. 'Did you tell her you were looking for the head to tell her about the graffiti?'

'Er, no.'

'Did you tell her you were looking for the head to tell her something else?' Riley asked.

'No.'

Amirah threw her hands up in exasperation. 'What did you tell her?'

'I couldn't think of anything! I just started getting really hot and panicky.'

Poor Thunder. He can't think straight when someone starts firing questions at him.

'You could have said you were lost, or anything; if you'd made out it was a mistake they couldn't have told you off.'

Thunder squirmed. 'I think I must've looked like I was expecting to be told off.'

It's true that when Thunder's been naughty he always looks completely guilty.

'Did you mention the club?' Amirah asked.

'I absolutely did not.' Thunder put his hand on his chest. 'Cross my heart.'

'I told you he wouldn't,' I said.

'So what did you say?' Riley asked.

'I told her it was just a dare.'

'Oh, great!' Amirah snapped. 'So you didn't tell her about our dare club, you just told her it was a dare. Did you happen to mention us lot as well?'

'No! I swear I never did.'

I completely believed him but Amirah wasn't going to let this go. 'Mrs Hamilton must have asked you who dared you.'

'She did.' Thunder looked pleased with himself. 'But I told her that I dared myself.'

Amirah burst out laughing. 'Oh, that's good. She probably let you go in the end because she thought you were too much of a moron to get any sense out of.'

Thunder's pleased expression melted away.

'Hey,' I said. 'Leave off Thunder. He hasn't told on us and I bet Mrs Hamilton tried to make him. I think he did a good job of keeping quiet.'

Thunder looked at me gratefully. 'I honestly didn't say anything about you lot. In the end, Mrs Hamilton said I could go to the exclusion room for the afternoon to think about what a silly waste of time dares are.'

'Waste of time my butt,' I said. 'These dares are the best fun I've had in ages.' Thinking about Adrenaline Club had really helped keep my mind off rugby, even if I was still missing it a bit.

And then, even though I'd already told them all about how I'd nabbed my blue slip, I went over the highlights again.

When they'd all gasped and oohed, Amirah said, 'I'm quite hot. Are you guys hot?'

I didn't think it was hot. The sun was out but it was still cool enough for a jumper. Then she pulled something papery out of her bag and fanned herself.

It was a blue slip.

'No way!' I said. 'When did you get that?'

She propped herself up on her elbows. 'Yesterday.'

Thunder looked miserable. 'How did you do it?'

'Mrs Hamilton teaches a lesson on Friday afternoon . . .'

'That was my idea,' I said.

Amirah ignored the interruption. 'So I waited till she was doing that then I went up to her secretary and told her that the head had sent me to get a worksheet she'd left on her desk. I walked right in and out again.'

Thunder sucked in his breath. He was clearly impressed.

'But what about the worksheet?' I asked. 'Didn't the secretary ask you where it was when you came back out?'

Amirah smiled. 'I had it hidden up my jumper when I went in. I took it out before I came back out.'

'That was clever,' Riley said.

He and Thunder were staring at Amirah like she was a genius or something. 'Not that clever,' I said. 'What if the secretary says something to the head about it?'

Amirah looked sideways at me. 'What if your prefect says something?'

'The head spends more time talking to her secretary than she does the prefects,' I pointed out.

Amirah pushed herself into a sitting position. 'Exactly. If the secretary was going to say something about it, she would have done it by now.'

'I think you were both pretty clever,' Riley said.

'And daring,' Thunder said.

Amirah's face softened. She gave me a thumbs-up.

I realised it was true that both of us had done well. 'You had a good plan,' I said to her.

'I got the waiting for her to be teaching bit from you,' she admitted.

I grinned at her.

Amirah opened a packet of crisps and passed them round. 'Tell you what I thought about doing: I was going to get myself deliberately sent to the head but I thought you might say that was cheating.'

I took another crisp. 'Yeah, it would be.'

'How could you get yourself deliberately sent?' Thunder asked.

Amirah pulled a face. 'What, like you've never been there? Normally your problem is staying out of there.'

Thunder nodded. 'But what were you going to do?'

'Oh, I don't know,' Amirah said. 'I can get into trouble just for opening my mouth. Maybe I would have told Mr Chadwick what I really think of him.'

'That would be fun,' I said. 'I can't believe that there are actually teachers like him. You would think that when he was doing his training and taking tests and stuff that someone would have decided he was too mean and horrible to be a teacher.'

Riley looked startled. 'Do teachers have to do tests?'

I looked in the crisp packet but they were all gone. 'Yeah, you actually have to know quite a lot of stuff to be a teacher.'

Riley blinked a bit.

I searched in my pockets for something else to eat. 'And it's not just about the thing that you teach, you have to learn about how to manage children and how they develop and things like that.'

'Chloe's mum and dad are teachers,' Thunder said.

'My dad *was* a teacher. He's an inspector now. And one of the things that he looks for in a classroom is the relationship between the teacher and the students. The teacher is supposed to understand us and support our learning.'

Riley looked like his eyes might pop. This was clearly news to him.

Amirah snorted. 'Mr Chadwick needs to try a bit harder to understand us. He could understand that we don't want to be shouted at all lesson or told that we're lazy.'

'Yeah,' Thunder said. 'And he doesn't support anything.'

'Except his huge backside,' I said. 'He keeps that supported because he never gets out of his chair.'

It's completely true. Other teachers move around their classroom. They look over your shoulder to check you're doing the work right, or they crouch down beside you to explain something. Mr Chadwick never moves from behind his desk.

'Seriously,' Amirah said. 'That's so true. For the first term he taught us I thought he didn't have legs.'

'I thought he was a merman,' I said.

We cracked up.

'Or one of those half-man, half-horse things!' Thunder laughed especially hard at his own joke.

'Sometimes I think I should make it an Adrenaline Club dare to teach Mr Chadwick a lesson,' I said.

'Like what?' Thunder asked.

I blew air between my lips making a raspberry noise while I thought about it. 'I don't know, just something to annoy him.'

Thunder had to go quite soon after that because his mum was making him go shopping for new school uniform as part of his punishment, but I spent the afternoon thinking about dares that would serve Mr Chadwick right.

CHAPTER ✿ TWENTY-THREE

The next morning the doorbell rang, so I abandoned my breakfast Cornish pasty and went to answer the door. Ella's friends, Kayleigh and Ashandra, were standing there.

'Hi, Chloe,' Ashandra said. 'We've come to pick up Ella.'

I opened the door wider so they could come in. 'Elllllla!' I shouted up the stairs.

'Coming! Just getting my purse!' she called back.

'Where are you lot going this morning?' I asked.

'Just to the shops,' Kayleigh said. 'We might get a milkshake.'

'In Fluffy's?'

They nodded.

'I love their Funky Monkey shakes,' I said. 'I could drink them all day.'

'We thought Ella needed cheering up,' Ashandra said. 'She's been worrying about—'

'The Student Council assembly,' I finished. 'I know.'

Ashandra rearranged her scarf. 'I told her that she should just say she doesn't want to do it.'

'I said she could pretend to be sick on that day,' Kayleigh said.

We all knew that Ella wouldn't do either of those things.

Then I thought of something. 'Hey, maybe you guys could help her.'

'What, like, write her speech?' Kayleigh asked.

I'd seen the pages of notes that Ella had already made for her speech. 'I think she's probably got that covered, but you could practise it with her. You both like talking, don't you?'

Kayleigh laughed. 'Yeah, especially Ashandra, she never shuts up!'

Ashandra smacked Kayleigh on the arm, 'Chloe means in front of people, like Ella's got to do in the assembly.'

Kayleigh shrugged. 'I don't mind it. And Ashandra's always doing it. She loves being in charge, don't you?'

Ashandra pretended to look cross with Kayleigh. 'Only because I like to make sure my group does a good job.'

'So you two could give her some tips?' I asked.

They looked at each other and smiled. 'Definitely,' Ashandra said. 'We could do a practice with her.'

Kayleigh's eyes lit up with an idea. 'Maybe we could even ask Miss Espinoza if we can go in the hall so she can practise saying it on the stage.'

'That's a good idea,' I said. Then I heard Ella on the landing. 'Anyway,' I said loudly, 'you should definitely try a Funky Monkey. It's chocolate and banana and it's amazing.'

'Kayleigh doesn't like bananas,' Ella said, coming down the stairs.

'I don't like the way they feel in your mouth,' Kayleigh said. 'I don't mind the flavour; it's the squishiness that's the problem.'

And they went out of the door talking about whether banana sweets have actually got any real banana in. I hoped Ella would have a nice time and I hoped that they'd be able to help her feel better about this stupid assembly.

Lucy clattered down the stairs carrying a bin bag. She looked at me with a hopeful expression. Amelia had stuck firm to Lucy only being her tweenie twice a week so in between times Lucy kept pestering me and Ella to pay her to do jobs. She'd do pretty much anything for a bit of change.

I'd had my wellies cleaned, my pillows plumped and my pencils sharpened all for a pound. I was going to ask her to do my homework but I remembered my conversation with Amelia and I thought that might be a bit mean. Besides, Lucy's spelling is even worse than mine.

'Got any jobs, guvnor?' Lucy asked. She hadn't really got the hang of talking like a maid. She sounded more like a chimney sweep.

'You've done pretty much everything I can think of,' I said. 'Unless you want to clear out under my bed.'

'I'm not going under there,' she said. 'No one even knows what's under there.'

'She's right,' Amelia called from the sitting room. 'That's not a job for a child; she'd probably get her hand bitten off.'

So I decided to leave that job for when one of my sisters is more desperate for cash.

'What's in the bin bag?' I asked.

'Toys,' Lucy said. 'I don't want these ones any more. I'm tidying mine and Ella's room, so I can get some money from Mum.'

That didn't sound like a very Mum-ish thing. Mum thinks we should keep our rooms spotless just to show how willing we are to 'contribute to the upkeep of the family home'. 'Has she actually said she's going to pay you for tidying your own room?' I asked.

'Duh, no, first I tidy it, then when she's really pleased with me I'll ask her for a *donation* to my Mrs Partridge money.'

Sometimes I can't help but admire Lucy's methods.

'I want to have lots of cash ready,' Lucy said. 'When Mrs Partridge is feeling better I'm going to give it to her.'

I didn't quite know what to say to that. Dad had made it pretty clear that Mrs Partridge didn't have long to live. If Lucy wanted to give her money she was going to have to do it soon.

I gently took the bin bag out of her hand and had a look inside. 'You've got some quite good stuff in here,' I said. 'If you really want to make some money you ought to sell this lot online.'

So that's how I ended up spending the rest of my Sunday helping Lucy list her old toys. I made Lucy check with Mum first and then I spent a very boring couple of hours taking photos of My Little Ponies and Power Rangers.

CHAPTER 🍓 TWENTY-FOUR

On Monday night, Mum asked me to help put the rubbish out. While I was cramming the last bin bag into the wheelie bin she told me she was just going to knock on Mr Partridge's door and ask if there had been any improvement with Mrs Partridge. I went inside to join Lucy and Ella in the sitting room but Mum was back before I'd even got the TV switched on. I could tell by her face that it wasn't good news.

'Lucy,' Mum said. 'There's something I need to tell you.'

Ella looked at me and I looked at Ella and we were pretty sure that we knew what that something was.

'What is it?' Lucy asked. 'I'm doing a very important drawing here.'

'Just put your pens down for a minute.' Mum pulled out a chair and sat down next to Lucy at the table.

Lucy sighed loudly and made a big fuss about clicking all the lids on to her pens.

'I've just spoken to Mr Partridge and ... oh, sweetheart, I'm so sorry but Mrs Partridge has died.'

Nobody said anything. I was holding my breath.

'Okay,' Lucy said. 'Can I finish my drawing now?'

'Lucy!' Ella said. I could see she was shocked. So was I. Someone dying is sad but Lucy didn't seem to care at all.

'Do you understand, darling?' Mum asked. 'Mrs Partridge has died. She won't be getting better and she won't be coming home.'

'I know what dying is,' Lucy said, looking at her pens instead of Mum.

Mum frowned. 'Well, if you have any questions or if you feel sad then you know you can talk to me, don't you?'

'I've got a question.'

Mum seemed relieved. 'Yes, love?'

'Do you know where my blue pen is?'

Mum opened her mouth and then shut it again.

She looked at Lucy as if she was searching for something in her face. 'I don't know where your pen is,' she said eventually. 'I'll keep an eye out for it.' She patted her on the shoulder. 'Remember what I said; if you want to talk about Mrs Partridge, I'm right here.'

But Lucy was already scribbling away with her black pen.

Lucy didn't say anything about Mrs Partridge for the rest of the evening. She went to bed as if it was just an ordinary day.

Ella came into the kitchen where I was making a cup of tea for me, Amelia and Mum. 'Do you want one?' I asked her, pointing at the mugs.

Ella shook her head. 'I'm worried about Lucy,' she said to Mum.

'Yeah, I'm worried too,' Amelia said. 'Worried that she is an actual alien. She doesn't seem to have human emotions. What kind of a way was that to react to someone dying?'

'Oh, Lucy has emotions,' Mum said. 'Lots of them. We see them all the time.'

'Are you sure?' I asked. 'Because mostly it's just shouting.'

Mum hesitated.

'She's very kind and loving with Kirsti,' Ella said.

That was true. Lucy was amazingly patient and gentle with the baby.

Mum nodded. 'And she was very happy when Chloe won her first rugby match and very sad when that vampire got killed in that film that you girls really shouldn't have let her watch. Lucy is a girl who feels things strongly.'

'I suppose that is true,' Amelia admitted. 'But that's why it's so cold that she doesn't care about Mrs Partridge.'

'I don't think that she doesn't care,' Mum said. 'I think she cares very much. She doesn't want to show it. Maybe not even to herself.'

I thought that what Mum was saying was pretty clever and probably true, because Lucy liked Mrs Partridge a lot, so she must care about her dying really. But it made my head spin. I don't understand the way people can feel one way and act another. It makes everything very confusing.

'I don't think people should hide their feelings inside like that,' I said.

Mum squeezed my arm. 'You're right; it's not good for you.'

'It's like trying to keep a fart in,' I said.

'Ewww! Chloe!' Amelia squealed.

But I didn't mean to be gross. I just meant that when you try and squeeze things tight inside it hurts.

'What's going to happen to Lucy?' Ella asked Mum. 'If she just keeps all her sad feelings inside, won't they get worse and build up and up until she explodes?'

'Like keeping a fart in,' I said again. That time I did mean to be gross because all this talking about feelings was getting depressing and I wanted to cheer everyone up.

Amelia whipped at me with a tea towel.

'I think Lucy will let out her feelings soon,' Mum said.

'Couldn't we do something to stop that happening?' Amelia asked. 'I don't want her to be sad.'

If Mum was surprised to hear Amelia worrying about Lucy she didn't show it. 'I don't think we should try to stop her feeling upset about Mrs Partridge. Sometimes you have to get really sad before you can start feeling happier.' She smiled round at us. 'When it happens, I know you girls will help her all you can.'

I really did want to help Lucy, but when you think about how loud and crazy Lucy is on an ordinary day, I was just a little bit afraid of what an exploding Lucy might be like.

CHAPTER ❦ TWENTY-FIVE

'I can't believe it! I just can't believe it,' Amelia said, storming into Dad's kitchen on Wednesday evening and slapping her phone down on the table in the middle of the cards Lucy and I were using to play *Cheat*.

'Tell us what it is,' I said, 'and then we can tell you whether it's believable or not.'

Amelia's eyes were hard and her mouth was twisted. 'I didn't get the part. I'm not going to be Amy in *Little Women*.'

'I can believe that,' Lucy said. 'You probably weren't very polite. Granny's always telling us that grumpy people don't get things they want.'

'Granny's always telling *you* that because you are a very rude little girl,' Amelia snapped.

I was shocked because since Lucy had heard that

Mrs Partridge had died we'd all been trying to be nice to her, even Amelia; *especially* Amelia.

I thought it was a good idea to get the conversation back on track. 'I'm really sorry you didn't get the part,' I said to Amelia. 'You would have been good at it.'

'I would! I know that sounds like I'm showing off, but I am good at singing and I did a brilliant audition. I know I was the best because I heard all the other girls too. They gave it to that Gabrielle girl from Community Choir. She doesn't even want to be a singer!'

'Is she any good?' I asked.

Amelia bunched up her mouth like she was trying to stop rude words escaping. 'Well,' she said eventually, 'if I'm really honest, I suppose she is quite good. But ... I really thought I'd get the part, Clo.'

And she looked at me and she stopped sounding like someone who thinks they're the best in the world and just sounded like someone who was very disappointed.

I knew what that felt like. It still hurt every time I thought about rugby camp and what I was going to miss out on. 'I'm sorry,' I said again. 'Sometimes even when you're the best they don't choose you.'

She sat down and slumped against my shoulder. 'It's not fair.'

The only thing I could say was, 'I know.'

Later on, while the three of us were clearing up after tea, Amelia told Suvi that she hadn't got the part. I waited for Suvi to say something sympathetic. Instead she asked, 'What does this Gabrielle girl look like?'

Amelia narrowed her eyes. 'What's that got to do with it? What matters is how she sings.'

'I think for a show on stage, the person who is choosing will be looking at faces.'

'She's small and blonde. Pretty.' The word 'pretty' came out as a growl.

'I see,' Suvi said.

Amelia put down a couple of forks with a clatter. 'No, you don't see. Just because she's good-looking doesn't mean she should get the part.'

Suvi carried on calmly washing dishes. 'In the book, Amy is described as small and blonde and pretty, isn't she?'

Amelia snatched up another plate to dry. 'So? I'm not exactly a heifer, am I? I could have passed for a pretty little girl, couldn't I?'

'For sure,' Suvi said in her gentle voice. 'I'm only saying that maybe this girl was a perfect fit for Amy.'

Amelia's head snapped up. That was the wrong thing to say. 'That's right, she's a perfect fit and I'm just rubbish.'

'I did not s—'

'You're basically saying I'm too ugly and ginormous to play the role, thanks a lot.'

'That is not what I am saying to you.'

There was a long silence. I hate it when Amelia gets cross with Suvi. She hadn't done it for ages, but now there was that horrible tense atmosphere like there used to be at Dad's when he and Suvi first got together. I racked my brains to think of a joke to tell.

'Amelia, Chloe,' Suvi said. 'Can you think of something Lucy would enjoy doing this weekend? I think she is very sad about her friend, Mrs Partridge.'

Amelia stared at her. 'Oh my God! You completely and utterly don't give a monkey's about me, do you? I'm actually really upset, in case you hadn't noticed. You probably don't even know what that's like, do you? Because no matter what happens you just go on talking in your stupid non-excited voice. Do you even feel anything about anything?'

Both my mum and my dad would have had plenty to say to Amelia about all of that, probably

165

in quite shouty voices. But Suvi just said, 'I think you should go and calm down now.'

'Oh, I'm going,' Amelia said in a not-at-all-calm way. 'I'm not staying where I'm not wanted.'

She threw down her tea towel and she stomped out of the kitchen, down the hallway and right out of the front door, slamming it behind her.

I looked at Suvi.

'It's so hard to understand Amelia,' she said to me. 'I wish she would speak more loudly. Do think that maybe she is a little upset?'

I burst out laughing and so did Suvi.

When she'd calmed down she put a hand on my arm. 'I shouldn't have said that.' She looked a bit horrified with herself. 'I am not laughing at Amelia; I know that she is having a hard day. It's just . . .'

'Sometimes she goes off like a firework.'

'Yes. And when it stops you are so amazed that it didn't whoosh into your eye that you laugh from the relief.'

Suvi put a hand to her chest and I saw that she was shaking a little bit. Amelia was wrong; Suvi does feel things. She was upset.

I didn't know what to say. 'Where do you think she's gone?' I asked, to fill the quiet.

Suvi took a deep breath and smiled at me. 'We

will wait for half an hour, then we will telephone Lauren and your mother. I think she will go to one of them.'

I felt bad that Amelia was somehow blaming all this audition stuff on Suvi. 'I'm sorry she shouted at you,' I said.

Suvi patted my shoulder. 'I am sorry that she thinks I don't care.'

Before the half an hour was up, Dad arrived home and said he'd had a call from Mum saying that Amelia was with her and she'd bring her back when she'd calmed down.

I was in the kitchen having some juice when I heard Amelia come in. I tried to hear what she said to Dad and Suvi but their voices were too low. After a few minutes she came out to the kitchen.

'Hi,' I said.

'I just had to say sorry to Suvi,' she said. 'Give me some of that, I need something to take away the horrible taste in my mouth.' And she picked up my glass of juice and took a long swig.

I poured myself a fresh glass. 'Are you, then?'

'Am I what?'

'Sorry.'

She groaned. 'I suppose so. I shouldn't have got

so worked up. It's just that Suvi never reacts to anything. Sometimes I want to scream and scream until it makes her scream too.'

I looked at her over my glass. 'You're weird.'

She scowled at me. 'How would you feel if you were watching the most exciting game of rugby ever and England were losing and you were on the edge of your seat and the seconds were ticking away and then at the very last moment England scored a try and won the World Cup?'

This sounded like one of my daydreams, except in my version I'm the one scoring the try. 'I'd be dancing for joy,' I said.

'Exactly, you'd be whooping and shouting and then you'd look at Suvi and she would say, "This is nice."'

'Suvi doesn't support England.'

Amelia made a growling noise in her throat. 'You know what I mean, I just wish she'd show some emotion.'

I thought about Suvi laughing in that crazy, relieved, half-guilty way. 'I think she does sometimes.'

'Well, I've never seen her. She can't even have an argument. This is what I said to Mum – Suvi doesn't even care enough about me to shout back at me.'

'What did Mum say?'

'She said perhaps she cares about me enough to not shout back.'

That was a very good point. I thought Amelia was being too harsh. Suvi had put up with a lot of yelling and whining from Amelia. 'Maybe Mum's right, it must be quite hard work because you are really annoying when you're in a bad mood. It's pretty nice of Suvi not to start telling you off.'

Amelia flopped over the counter. 'I guess. Mum says that we're all so loud and shouty that I'm not appreciating the fact that Suvi shows she cares in different ways.'

I thought about how Suvi had been determined to help me set up the girls' rugby training. She was actually properly angry that my PE teacher told me not to bother about it. And it wasn't just about me and the rugby squad; she told all of us that we should never accept being treated differently to boys. She definitely cares about that. Plus, I've noticed that even though Ella is super shy, Suvi has somehow made friends with her. And she wanted to do something nice for Lucy this weekend. 'I think that's true,' I said. 'There are loads of ways that Suvi is kind to us.'

Amelia shrugged. 'I'm still waiting to see one of these ways.'

CHAPTER ❤ TWENTY-SIX

The next morning Thunder pulled me into a corner during registration.

'Can we have a meeting of the, uh, you know what?' He waggled his eyebrows.

'Do you mean Adrenaline Club?'

'Yes,' he whispered.

I looked over at Mrs Montgomery to make sure she hadn't noticed Thunder. If she saw him trying so hard not to draw attention, she'd know straightaway that we were up to something, but she was busy sorting out a pile of papers.

'What's the rush?' I asked.

'I've got something to say.' His face split into a wide smile.

'All right. How about on the field at breaktime?'

He rubbed his chin. 'It's not very secret.'

'Well, I was going to suggest the underground bunker but we've got to get back in time for maths.'

He laughed, before he remembered he was trying to be quiet and spy-like so he clapped a hand over his mouth. Then he had to take it off again so he could say, 'All right, on the field, but right down the end by the trees so no one will see what . . . I mean, no one will see.'

There was definitely something going on. 'What's this all about?'

'You'll see,' he said, and grinned his wide-mouthed grin again.

So I had to sit through English and history being totally bored. I could have had a little nap, but every time I started to drift off Thunder gave me a nudge and pulled his secret-agent face; by the time the bell went for break, I was dying of curiosity.

We rounded up Amirah and Riley and headed for the far end of the field.

'Come on, then, Thunder,' I said, before I'd even got my breaktime snack out. 'Quit winking and giggling and tell us what you've got to say.'

'It's not exactly saying, it's more showing.'

Amirah groaned. 'Oh my days, you're not going to try that trick where you take your pants off without taking your trousers off again, are you?

171

Because last time you did that I saw way more of your backside then I ever want to again.'

'Nah,' said Thunder. 'It's not that . . .' He fished about in his pocket and pulled something out. 'It's this.'

It was a pen.

'It's a pen,' Amirah said.

I looked at it more closely. It was a purple pen.

'That is never Mr Chadwick's, is it?' Amirah asked.

Riley face lit up. 'No way!'

I didn't say anything.

Thunder chuckled. 'It is his.' He was going pink with delight. 'I got it yesterday. Guess he won't be able to write any more dumb comments on my homework.'

'He'll probably manage,' Amirah said. 'Since that isn't the only pen in the world. But it's still pretty cool.'

I had a sick feeling in my stomach.

Thunder looked at me. 'It's like you said, isn't it? The Adrenaline Club needed to teach Mr Chadwick a lesson. Such a shame that his purple pen just disappeared.'

That wasn't at all what I'd meant. The queasy feeling was bubbling inside me. I snatched the pen out of his hand. 'It'll just have to reappear.'

'What are you on about?' Amirah asked.

I couldn't believe that they all thought this was okay. 'It's a teacher's pen! You can't just take it.'

Thunder's grin dropped off his face. 'But you said . . .'

'I meant maybe we could start humming in his lesson or . . . or put salt in his coffee or something! I didn't mean you should steal from him. You've got to put it back.'

Thunder had lost his pink cheeks. 'I can't.'

'What's the big deal about taking stuff?' Amirah asked. 'We took blue slips.'

I threw my hands up. This wasn't at all like a little bit of paper that no one cared about. 'But this belongs to him! It's not like a blue slip; this is one of his actual things. How would you feel if someone helped themselves to something of yours?'

'I still don't know why you're making such a fuss,' Amirah said huffily.

I didn't exactly know myself. I knew it was only a pen, but somehow it felt like things had gone too far. Maybe I felt bad because Thunder thought I wanted him to do it so this was sort of my fault, or maybe it was because it reminded me of when I was in Year Three and one of the big kids took my felt tips and I never got them back. I knew I was overreacting, but it just felt wrong to me.

'I don't think we should take anyone's stuff,' I said.

Thunder chewed the cuff of his jumper. 'I didn't think about it like that.'

He looked really sad. When I thought about how excited he'd been about showing us the stupid pen, I felt sorry for the great melon.

I let out a long, heavy breath. 'Don't worry. I'll think of a way of putting it back.'

That seemed to make him feel a bit better.

I folded my arms. 'But can we all agree that in Adrenaline Club we do cool stuff that is daring and scary and maybe a bit rule-breaking, but we *do not* take other people's things? Ever.'

Amirah muttered a bit but the other two nodded.

I looked at each one of them in turn. 'And if you do, I will slice open your heads and steal your brains to see how you like it when someone messes with something that belongs to you.'

CHAPTER ❤ TWENTY–SEVEN

It was all very well saying I'd put the pen back, but I wasn't entirely sure how to do it. I didn't have chemistry until Monday and I wanted to get it over with before then. Mr Chadwick's lab was always locked unless he was in it, and if he was there he never left his desk where he keeps his purple pen.

I wondered about slipping it in his bag or his pocket. But I'd never seen him with a bag and the idea of getting close enough to Mr Chadwick to put something in his pocket was just too gross to think about.

I worried about what to do all through maths. It seemed crazy that I was tying myself up in knots about this, but I wanted to make a point to the others; I knew it was the right thing to do even though Mr Chadwick probably hadn't even missed his stupid pen. He probably just thought he'd lost it.

That's when it hit me.

If Mr Chadwick thought he'd lost his pen, then why didn't I find it for him? I was so pleased with my idea that it must have been showing all over my face because Mr Ireland crept up on me and told me that for someone who had done remarkably little work I looked spectacularly smug.

I didn't tell him that for someone with such large amounts of nostril hair he seemed surprisingly keen to poke his nose over people's shoulders.

But I thought it.

At lunchtime I gobbled my lunch and then scooted off to the lab where, luckily, Mr Chadwick was sitting at his desk eating a Pot Noodle.

I walked right on in. 'Um, Mr Chadwick?'

'Yes?' He didn't look up from his snack.

I took that as an invitation to come closer and shuffled up to his desk. 'About our homework.'

He groaned, put down his fork and sort of rolled his head up as if it was a huge effort just to look at me.

'What homework? I teach hundreds of navy blue blobs like you, in a number of classes, where I set a variety of stimulating homeworks, most of which remain undone. You'll have to be a little more specific.'

I was starting to regret even bothering to try to get his pen back to him. 'I'm in 8NM'

'Good for you. Is there any danger of us reaching the end of this scintillating chat? Only, I've got another bunch of knuckle-draggers arriving shortly and obviously I'll need to set up the lab and compose my thoughts before they arrive.' He snorted. 'Either that or I would like to finish this Pot Noodle.'

'Er, I was just wondering . . . when's it due in?'

'When's your next chemistry lesson?'

'Monday.'

'That's when it's due then. At your next lesson, as has been the case for every homework you have ever had with me.'

I nodded. 'Right. Good. I'll make sure I get it done.'

He was already eating again. He'd splattered a bit of sauce across his chin.

'Oh!' I said, bending down and reaching under his desk 'What's this?' I slid his pen out of my sleeve and stood up again. 'It's a pen.'

He held out his hand and I handed it to him.

'You must have dropped it,' I said.

He gave me a long look out of his half-closed eyes.

I turned and scarpered.

I rushed off to French. Thunder had saved me a seat.

'I put back Mr Chadwick's pen,' I told him.

Thunder flinched. 'Was it okay?'

'It was really easy.'

'Do you think he suspected anything?'

I leant back in my chair. 'Why would he? Anyway, I think I'm actually a very good actor. I don't know why people go to special drama schools to learn it. I just make things up and say them.'

'What exactly did you say?'

'I asked him when our homework was due and then I pretended to find his pen on the floor.' I was pretty pleased with how clever I'd been.

Thunder was still looking at me. 'Didn't he think that was weird?'

'Mr Chadwick's whole world is weird. I don't think he'd notice any extra bits. The point is that the pen has been returned and we're no longer in danger.'

'I thought you liked danger.'

'I like things that are exciting,' I said. 'But I don't want to do anything that's totally wrong.' I didn't get to explain any more than that because our teacher came in and we had to stop talking.

I thought I was done with the whole thing, but later, when I was in bed, there was a little voice in my head that was saying it was kind of amazing that I had just mentioned about Mr Chadwick being annoying and deserving a lesson, and Thunder actually went and did something about it. If I was an army general, I bet Thunder would follow me into battle. In fact, I probably wouldn't even have to go into battle myself because I could just command him to get out there and do it and off he'd go. I wouldn't do that, though. My dad always says that you shouldn't ask people to do jobs that you're not prepared to do yourself.

CHAPTER ❤TWENTY-EIGHT

On Friday morning, I was cramming stuff into my bag ready for Dad's house that night when I heard shouting coming from the kitchen. A lot of shouting goes on in our house. Amelia shouts if someone has breathed on her make-up, or left a tiny bit of their hair in her sandwich (it's not like I put it there on purpose) but it wasn't Amelia because she came into our bedroom looking for her Community Choir music.

'I didn't know if you'd keep going after you didn't get that part,' I said.

Amelia shrugged. 'It's not their fault I didn't get it. Anyway, Lauren and I like singing at Community Choir; everyone there is so ...'

'NOOOOOO!' We heard Lucy scream from the kitchen.

'. . . relaxed,' Amelia finished. 'Unlike this house.'

Which seemed a lot like what Suvi had said to her but I didn't get to point that out because there was more wailing from downstairs, and I thought I'd better go and check Lucy wasn't beating Mum with a saucepan.

In the kitchen Mum was wearing her patient look and Lucy was throwing a ballet shoe across the room while ranting.

'. . . then she said that I was grumpy! And she made us all stop and look at Imogen's *pas de chat* and even though I was jumping much higher than her and th—'

'Just take a deep breath, sweetheart,' Mum said. 'I'm sure Madame Donna didn't mean to upset you.'

Madame Donna is Lucy's ballet teacher and obviously Lucy wasn't very happy with her.

'She did mean to upset me!' Lucy shouted. 'You don't call people grumpy and a silly sausage to be nice!'

'Why are you shouting about it now?' I asked. 'You didn't say anything about it after your lesson on Saturday.'

'I didn't remember it then. I'm remembering it now!'

Mum was picking up Lucy's ballet things, which seemed to have been thrown around the room. 'Just pop these in your bag for Dad's,' she said to Lucy.

Lucy snatched her leotard out of Mum's hand. 'It's all scrumpled!' Lucy whined.

I was pretty sure that you could have given Lucy a gold medal right at that moment and she would have said it was too shiny.

'The creasy bits will drop out while you're wearing it,' I said.

'That's not what happens with you,' Lucy said. 'You always look like you've been sleeping in your clothes. Sleeping in a stinky troll cave.'

I quite liked the idea of hanging out with trolls. I bet they know some great wrestling moves. 'Cool,' I said.

But Mum didn't think it was cool. 'Lucy, you need to calm down. I know you're upset about Madame Donna and ... other things, but there's no need to be rude to Chloe.'

'I don't mind,' I said. 'Do you want some toast, Lucy?'

'No! I don't want any stupid toast.'

'Lucy!' Mum pushed her into a chair. '*Calm down*.'

Lucy dropped her leotard on the floor. 'I don't

want to! Madame Donna's mean and I'm not taking my ballet things to Dad's because I'm never going back to ballet again!'

Mum put a hand on her shoulder. 'Let's just give it some time, shall we? You've been worked up over something at ballet before but it's always blown over, hasn't it?'

'I'm not going back.'

'I think we'll wait and see how you feel next week. I've already paid a full term's fees and we haven't got money to throw away.'

Lucy suddenly jerked upright, eyes wide with horror. 'Mrs Partridge's money!' she said. 'The money from my toys and everything. I made all that money for her. How can I give it to her now?'

I looked at Mum. I couldn't think what she could possibly say to Lucy when she was in this mood. I thought the explosion might be on its way.

Mum sat down in the chair next to Lucy. 'You can't give it to her now,' she said gently. 'But perhaps you could use it to do something that Mrs Partridge would have liked. Mr Partridge is having a collection for cancer research; you could give it to that.'

Lucy looked furious. 'No! I'm not giving it to him. Mrs Partridge didn't like cancer. She said it was a ruddy waste.'

'Don't say ruddy.' Mum took a deep breath. 'No, of course she didn't like cancer. That's why her son is collecting money to fund research – that means scientists try to find out everything they can about cancer, including how to cure it.'

Lucy's forehead creased. 'They're going to get a way to cure it? Why haven't they done it before?'

Poor Mum was struggling to know what to say.

'I think they have already been trying to find a cure,' I said.

'Scientific research takes years,' Mum added. 'But they are making progress; all the time they're finding out more about cancer and how to treat different types.'

Lucy eyes went hard. 'They didn't treat Mrs Partridge. They didn't care about her at all!'

Mum put an arm around her. 'They tried, love. I promise you that the doctors did their very best to help Mrs Partridge. The thing is that she was very old and bodies can't keep going for ever.'

'Well, they should! It's stupid. It's stupid that people die! It's a ruddy waste!' She was so angry that her body was all stiff and her fists were clenched. 'It's not fair!' she shouted.

And then, finally, Lucy started to cry.

Mum scooped her onto her lap and rocked her back and forth. Lucy howled. Eventually, her rigid body relaxed into Mum's hug and she cried and cried.

I could almost feel all her anger and sadness just oozing out of her along with the tears, and even though it was horrible to see her so miserable, I was relieved that she'd finally found a way to let out how upset she was.

My mum was right: sometimes you have to get very sad before you can feel happier.

CHAPTER ❤TWENTY-NINE

'Have you even thought of a new dare?' Amirah asked Thunder, when we were all gathered under a tree in the park sheltering from the rain on Sunday morning.

Thunder shot a panicked look at me. He'd already told me that he couldn't think of a single thing. 'Thunder's letting me come up with his dare,' I said.

'Why?' Amirah asked. 'It's supposed to be his turn.' She pointed a finger at Thunder. 'Can't you think of anything?'

'Of course he can. He's got loads of ideas, but I really wanted to do this one today.'

Amirah rolled her eyes. 'All right fine, tell us what it is.'

'We're going to jump off the stone bridge into

the river,' I said. I'd been wanting to do it for ages, but Ella was always talking me out of it.

'Cool!' Thunder said.

'Won't we get wet?' Riley asked.

'We're already wet,' Amirah said. Then she asked, 'How high is this bridge?'

'You'll see when we get there,' I said. We left the park and went back the way I'd come but turned off before my road and down the lane towards the river. As we got closer and the bridge came into view, I could see Amirah was unimpressed, but once we were actually on the bridge, leaning over looking down into the water, her face changed. Things feel a lot higher when you're thinking about jumping off them.

'We're going to get drenched,' Riley said.

'Nah, it only comes up to your knees,' Thunder said.

I started undoing my laces. 'Roll up your trousers, it'll hardly show, then.'

Riley looked worried. 'If it's really shallow, is that enough to, you know, break your fall?'

'It's not a fall,' I said. 'It's a jump, and it's not that far. Just remember to bend your knees.'

'Bend my knees,' he repeated. His face was deadly serious.

Thunder slapped him on the shoulder. 'Cheer up, it'll be a laugh. Who's going first?'

I'd got my trainers and socks off and rolled my jeans up as high as I could get them. 'I'll go,' I said. I gave Riley my phone to hold, then I swung my legs over the edge so I was sitting on the parapet. I looked down at the water. It did seem a fair way off. I felt my heart beating faster. It felt good. Like when I'm playing an important rugby match and I'm about to kick a try. I was going to do it. I took a deep breath and pushed off.

'Geronimo!' I shouted.

For an instant I felt like I was hanging in the air, then there was a rush and I landed squarely in the freezing water, my feet sinking into the sandy-mud stuff on the bottom. I splashed over to the side and climbed out. The others were yelling and cheering.

'It's great!' I said, running back up for my shoes.

'Awesome!' Thunder said. 'You did a really big jump.'

'Bet I can do a bigger one,' Amirah said. She was crouching on the edge of the bridge on her bare feet, rather than sitting like I had. Slowly, she stood up. I was just wondering if that was a good idea, since the edge was curved and wet and slippery, when she bent her legs ready to jump.

Then everything happened very quickly.

As she was pushing off, her right foot skidded out

in front of her so that instead of launching forward, she tipped back, crunching her arm beneath herself against the bridge. I tried to reach out and grab her, but it was too late and she slid away from my grasp.

I leant over the bridge and watched her falling, legs and arms all over the place. She landed on her side in the water below.

You always like to think that you'll be the kind of person who is cool and calm in an emergency. But when something really bad happens, you don't have complete control over your body. For a moment, I felt like I was trapped in treacle and I couldn't move. The only thing I could see was Thunder's mouth with his lips going, 'Oh no, oh no,' over and over again. But my nana used to tell me that in an emergency what you have to do is not think about what's happened, but what you're going to do now because taking action is the best way to help yourself or someone else. So I knew I had to get Amirah out of the water.

'It's all right,' I called to her. My voice came out weird. Amirah didn't answer. She wasn't moving. I pointed to my phone, which Riley was still holding, but he was staring very hard at Amirah.

'Call an ambulance,' I said to him. He looked at me in surprise.

'Call an ambulance,' I said again.

'Okay,' he said. 'Okay, okay.'

I scrambled down the bank. Amirah was still in a heap with her face down in the water. Was she going to drown?

I leapt into the water and thank goodness, Amirah's head finally lifted. She spat out a load of water and took a huge gaspy breath.

'It's okay,' I said. 'I'm coming.'

I waded further into the water. This time I had my trainers on. It was freezing and my legs didn't seem to be properly connected to my brain. I had to concentrate really hard to keep them moving. 'I'm coming,' I said again. 'I'm going to get you out.'

But Amirah wasn't looking at me; she was making this high-pitched moaning sound.

When I finally reached her, she said, 'Oh my God, look at my arm.'

Her right arm was twisted back in a way arms really shouldn't be. I almost started to panic again. I was afraid to touch her. I wanted my mum so much. My mum would know exactly what to do. She'd get her out of the water. So I moved to her good side and gripped her under the elbow. 'We have to get you to the bank,' I said.

She didn't move.

'Come on,' I said. 'Take a step.'

But she was frozen. I slid my hand around her waist, being careful to avoid her limp arm. Then I bent my knees and lifted her up into my arms. Amirah is quite a lot smaller than me, but it's pretty difficult to carry even quite a light person when you're walking across an uneven riverbed. I was terrified I was going to drop her and do more damage.

By the time I'd worked my way to the edge of the water, Thunder was there and he took her out of my arms into his.

We sat her down on the grass and I made Thunder take off his hoodie to wrap her in. She was shaking really hard.

'The ambulance said they'd be here soon,' Riley said.

Then there was a horrible silence, until Amirah started making little whimpering noises like a dog that's got its paw trapped.

'Hey, Amirah,' I said, putting my arm around her. 'Remember when we played rugby against that girls' school? And that snobby girl called me a pauper?'

I couldn't tell if she was listening but I kept talking about rugby and then about Mr Chadwick. I felt like an idiot. I sounded like an idiot. I'm sure even Amirah was wondering what the hell I was going on about but I had this idea that if I kept talking somehow it might help to stop her from flipping out or looking at her twisted arm. So I just kept on and on; the boys helping me along a bit and Amirah looking at us as if she didn't completely understand English and then finally, finally, after what felt like the longest minutes of my life, we heard the ambulance in the distance. It was such a relief when they pulled up and the paramedic jumped out. I've never been so pleased to see a grown-up. They took charge straightaway, firing questions at us and walking Amirah into the ambulance.

'You'd all better go home and get dry. Now,' was the last thing the lady said to us before they drove away.

CHAPTER 🍓 THIRTY

Before I'd even got back to Dad's, I'd started shaking. By the time I got in the door I was shaking so hard that it was a struggle to get my shoes off.

I was squelching my way up the stairs when Suvi appeared.

'Chloe? What has happened?'

I was pretty sure I was in big, big trouble. Not only was I dripping river water all over her super-clean cream carpet, I was also going to have to explain about Amirah's arm. Amirah's arm that was broken because of me.

I'd basically broken someone's arm.

A sort of gulpy noise came out of me.

Suvi put her arms out and wrapped me in a hug. Then I properly started crying.

Dad came out into the hallway. 'What's al—'
He saw my snotty face. 'Clo? What's the matter?'

So I sobbed out the whole story to him and Suvi.
The club, the dares, the Ghost School, the blue
slips. Everything.

Dad looked pretty stern. 'The whole thing was
your idea?' he asked.

'Yes,' I said in a tiny voice.

'To me it seems that all of the friends wanted to
do this also,' Suvi said.

'But I thought of the dare,' I said.

Dad ran a hand over his face. 'I think the lot of
you have been very silly.'

I tried not to start howling again.

'I think what you need now is a bath,' Suvi said
and she went up to the bathroom and turned the
taps on.

I looked at Dad. I hated seeing him all sad and
disappointed with me. *Why did I have to be such an
idiot?*

'I'm really sorry,' I said. 'I didn't think it would
be dangerous.'

'That's the problem, Chloe, you don't think
enough about the consequences of your actions.'

Another tear escaped and rolled down my
cheek.

'I need to speak to your mother about this. And

I think I probably need to have a conversation with the parents of the other members of your club.'

My insides turned to ice. Now I was getting everyone into trouble.

'But the first thing is for you to get clean and dry. We'll talk about this later.'

So I had my bath and Suvi made me a hot drink and brought me a biscuit, even though she doesn't really approve of biscuits.

Then I ate my tea without saying much to anyone and went to bed super early. I thought I was going to lie awake all night worrying, but actually I was exhausted, so I dropped off and slept right through till Dad woke me in the morning.

'What time is it?' I asked.

'It's nearly nine o'clock. I've rung school to tell them you'll be a bit late. I thought you needed the rest.'

I rubbed the sleep out of my eyes. I wondered if Amirah had slept okay or if she was in a lot of pain.

'Get your uniform on and then we need a chat,' Dad said.

It's not like I usually enjoy getting ready for school, but it was pretty horrible putting on my things knowing that there was A Chat coming next. I wondered if Dad was going to shout at me.

I thought shouting would probably be better than that disappointed face he pulled yesterday.

When I came down to the kitchen Dad pulled out a chair and I sat down on it.

'Is Amirah all right?' I asked. 'Did you speak to her mum?'

'Her arm is broken in two places.'

He let that sink in for a moment.

'Did you tell her mum I'm sorry?'

'You'll be telling Amirah that yourself.'

I nodded. 'I'll tell the others I'm sorry too.'

'Yes, you will. Fortunately for you, Amirah's mum doesn't seem to blame you. She says Amirah ought to have known better. In fact, having spoken to all the parents they seem to be in agreement that their children are responsible for their own stupid decisions.'

I felt super grateful for that.

Dad let out a long breath. 'Chloe, I understand that you were missing rugby and looking for some fun, but this wasn't the right way to go about it.'

'No,' I agreed.

'Your dares were spectacularly stupid. Imagine if you'd been caught in the primary school grounds! They might have thought you were trying to break in to steal things.'

'But we weren't! I'd never do that!'

'If you trespass after dark then that's the sort of impression you give.'

I hung my head. I hadn't thought what other people might think about what we were doing.

Dad ran a hand through his hair. 'The thoughtless, dangerous dares are one thing. Your mother and I are agreed that the real worry here is your role in all this.'

'My role,' I repeated, nodding my head. 'Wait, what do you mean my role?'

'You were the leader of this club, weren't you?'

'Yes. I thought up most of the dares.'

'It was more than that, though.'

'Was it? I tried to keep it equal. I remembered what you always say: I didn't expect anyone to do anything I wouldn't do.'

Dad groaned and covered his face with his hands.

'You did say that, didn't you?'

Dad dropped his hands to his lap. 'I did say it, but it doesn't really apply to irresponsible dares, and I think if you'd given it any thought at all then you would have known that. There are some things that you shouldn't be asking people to do at all.'

'But I didn't! I honestly didn't make anyone do anything. I never said they had to do it.'

'There are more ways of getting someone to do

197

something than coming right out and ordering them.'

'I didn't bully them into it either.'

'I believe you. You're a decent kid. You're also popular and funny and a charismatic leader.'

I didn't know what charismatic meant, but I was glad that the conversation had turned round to my good points.

'And that means that you've got a lot of influence. And with that influence comes responsibility. Other kids like you, some of them look up to you, they want to impress you and be your friend. Sometimes, without even knowing you're doing it, you're having an effect on the choices your friends make.'

I thought that was crazy. But then I remembered what Amirah had said about Thunder and Riley being prepared to do anything I asked. Maybe it was possible that the rest of the club had done things to make me happy. 'But I can't help that, can I? If I've got this invisible power then I can't control it, can I?'

'Actually, you can. You have to think about the example you're setting, the ideas you're supporting and how they might influence others.'

I did not like the sound of that. 'You're basically saying I have to be good all the time, aren't you?'

Dad snorted and I was relieved that the dead serious expression was finally gone from his face. 'I'm saying just think about the ideas you put in other people's heads.'

I thought hard. I really didn't want to be responsible for any more broken arms. Or even for anyone being put in the exclusion room.

'I can try,' I said slowly. 'But sometimes I don't even realise I'm doing something wrong. I mean, I knew it was a *bit* naughty, but I honestly thought it was okay if I was prepared to do it too.'

Dad shook his head. 'I wish I'd never said that. I guess it's true of some situations. The thing is, Clo, there are very few rules that apply to absolutely every situation. Except perhaps "do the right thing".'

I threw up my hands. That was not very helpful advice. 'How on earth am I supposed to know what the right thing is all the time?'

'You have to try to work it out for yourself.'

'That's hard.'

'It is. Sometimes I still don't know what the right thing to do is.'

I was surprised by that. It seemed liked being good was a difficult job. 'I'll have a go,' I said. 'I promise I will try.'

He smiled at me. 'I know you will. You always do.'

CHAPTER ❤ THIRTY-ONE

Dad dropped me off at school, five minutes into my second lesson. Thunder raised his eyebrows at me as I took my seat next to him, but we couldn't really speak until breaktime. Turned out his mum and dad had given him a long talking-to as well.

'They were already cross about the exclusion room, so now I'm grounded for two weeks.'

'I got no TV, no computer and no phone for three weeks,' I said.

Thunder winced. 'Riley's got to sort their garden out, which sounds okayish, but their garden is a complete jungle; it's going to take him for ever.'

He looked pretty depressed. I felt a wave of guilt wash over me. 'Listen, Thunder, I'm really sorry about all this.'

He looked up. 'It's not your fault.'

'It sort of is. Adrenaline Club was my stupid idea and then even when you said you didn't want to do stuff like sneaking into the head's office I persuaded you into it.'

Thunder shook his head. 'No, you didn't. You never said I had to.'

'I kind of made you feel like you ought to do it, though, didn't I? And that wasn't really fair.'

He shrugged. 'Maybe. I'm not blaming you. My mum says we were all daft.'

'She's right. I just wanted to say that in future, if I have any more daft ideas I'm not going to drag you into them. I'm not even going to drag myself into them. I'm going to save my brain for fun stuff that won't get us into trouble.'

'All right.'

'So are we cool?'

Thunder gave me a shove. ''Course. We're always cool.'

I felt a lot better after I'd had that conversation, even though I had to do it all over again at lunchtime with Riley. And there was still Amirah to talk to, but mostly, by the time I got home I was feeling ready to start putting the whole thing behind me.

Someone who clearly wasn't focusing on the future was Ella. She'd been deadly quiet all the way home and once we were there she hid herself away in her bedroom. I took her up a cup of tea and found her huddled on her bed.

'You okay?' I asked, putting her tea down on the bookshelf.

'I'm fine,' she said.

It wasn't at all hard to think of the right thing to do in this situation. I gave her a cuddle. 'Ella? You know that if you've got a problem you can tell me. I can probably help; apparently I'm a leader of young people.'

She burst out laughing. It was a nice sound.

'Nah, seriously,' I said, 'is it the assembly?'

She didn't say yes, but then she didn't say no.

'It is the assembly. You don't want to do it, do you?'

It was a bit of a strange way to have a conversation because I was filling in Ella's bits for her, but I could tell from her eyes that I was on the right track.

'I think you shouldn't do it,' I said.

Her eyes clouded so that was wrong. I knew why. 'You don't want to let them down, do you?'

Her head shook just a fraction.

I tried to think of a way round that. 'What if they could get someone else?'

'But I ought to try,' Ella burst out. 'You need to be good at speaking. It's important for jobs and things.'

I nearly laughed at that. I can't picture Ella doing any kind of job where she has to give speeches. I imagine her in some sort of lab, writing long lists of numbers on whiteboards.

'They honestly wouldn't mind if someone else did it, Ella.'

Her big eyes looked up at me.

'But you mind, don't you?'

She nodded.

I was starting to feel frustrated; it seemed so obvious to me: *I* would have no problem telling them I didn't want to do it, but then again *I* wouldn't have minded giving a speech in the first place.

That was it.

It was no good just trying to think of the right thing, it had to be the right thing for Ella. There was no way for her to get out of this without her feeling bad, so maybe she should just do it.

'How about this,' I said. 'You give the speech a go and once you've given it your best shot, then you tell Miss Espinoza that you don't want to be Student Council rep any more?'

Ella opened her mouth.

'Obviously you'd give her time to find a replacement. It's nearly half-term; she'll have a whole week to think of someone.'

Ella's shoulders relaxed and I knew we'd hit on the answer. To me, it still seemed harsh that she was going through with the speech when it was making her so nervous, but then I realised that's something pretty cool about Ella: she doesn't do what's easiest, she does what she thinks is right.

For a quiet, bookish girl she is actually pretty tough. I think I could learn a lot from her.

CHAPTER ✿ THIRTY-TWO

The next day, after school, I parcelled up all the toys Lucy had sold and Mum drove me to the Post Office to send them off. All together Lucy had made over seventy pounds. When you added on everything she'd made from tweenie-ing and the cakes and washing Dad's car, she had a ton of money. Except, of course, Mrs Partridge wasn't here for Lucy to give it to. I wondered what Lucy would do with it, but Lucy hadn't mentioned the toys since Mrs Partridge had died so I decided it might not be the best thing to ask her about it right now.

After the Post Office, Mum dropped me off at the hospital to see Amirah. Some people don't like hospitals but I don't mind them. They're always so busy. I think it would be good to work in a hospital. It must be quite dramatic being a doctor;

you never know who's going to come in next. One minute you're sorting out little Jonny's broken finger, and the next minute, in comes the victim of a shark attack spurting blood everywhere and you have to shout at everybody to save his life. If you've got to get out of your pyjamas in the morning to go to work, it really should be to do something exciting. I would get totally bored in an office where everybody did the same thing every day. Actually, I think I might like to work outside best. Maybe I could fly one of those air ambulances.

Amirah's mum had told my mum that Amirah was on Holly Ward, so I asked a lady at the big desk in the main entrance where that was. She sent me to the lifts to go up to the children's department on the seventh floor. When I got up there I had to ask again and they pointed me down a corridor and to the right.

When I saw the sign for Holly Ward, I had a quick panic. What if Amirah was really badly injured? What if she was angry with me? Then I spotted her in a bed by the window. Her arm was in a cast and she was looking at a magazine. I pulled myself up straight. If she *was* furious, the sooner I told her I was sorry, the better.

I strode up to her bed. 'I'm really sorry, Amirah. The whole Adrenaline Club thing was a stupid idea and I'm sorry I ever thought of it and I'm especially sorry that I suggested jumping off the bridge and I'm really super extra sorry that you broke your arm.' I let out a big breath.

Amirah blinked at me. 'Hello to you, too.'

'Oh. Yeah. Hi.'

She put down her magazine. 'Hi yourself.'

'But I am sorry.'

'That's nice. It's not like it's your fault, though.'

I sat down on the chair next to her bed. 'It was my idea.'

'You didn't exactly push me.'

'No, but . . .'

'Listen, I guess we've both decided no more Adrenaline Club, yeah?'

'Yes.'

'And maybe the next time one of us thinks she's got a great idea, the other one could tell them not to be an idiot.'

'I could do that.' I remembered Amirah talking to me after Thunder got caught in the head's office and I felt my face getting hot. 'Actually, you tried to do that with me already, didn't you?'

Amirah shrugged. 'That was just me worrying about the boys. I think maybe we have to worry a bit about ourselves, too.'

'Definitely.'

She nodded.

'Does your arm hurt?'

'Aches a bit.'

'What was it like when it broke?'

'I dunno, I felt really weird, like I was going to be sick. There was that bit . . .'

'Poking up! I know.' I shook my head. 'Arms should not look like that.'

'They had to operate on me to make it go back into position.'

She seemed kind of proud about that.

'Will you have a scar?' I asked.

'A little one.'

'Cool.'

Then we talked a bit about school and about what our parents had said to us, and I showed her a picture of the jungle garden that Riley's parents were expecting him to get under control.

She leant back on her pillows.

'I'd better get going,' I said. 'When are you coming home?'

'Tomorrow.'

I stood up. 'And how long will it be before the cast comes off?'

'Weeks. I tell you what, as soon as it does come off, I'm going straight back to rugby.'

I was not expecting that. 'Really?'

'Yeah. I miss it. I still wish I'd been picked for the camp, but maybe, you know ...' She pointed at her cast, 'Coach does have a point about us two not being the most sensible, reliable types.'

'I suppose,' I said. 'Well ... sorry again about, you know, everything.'

'It's fine,' she said. 'See you later.'

'Yeah, see you at school.'

I walked back towards the lifts. I'd been trying hard not to think about rugby and Coach but they were always in the back of my mind. I had to admit that what Amirah had said was true. It was pretty obvious to me now why Coach hadn't picked me for the camp: he didn't trust me not to muck around. And when you looked at the last couple of weeks, I couldn't really blame him.

I got the bus home. Mum was marking in the sitting room and the other three were in the kitchen, clearing up tea.

'We saved you some,' Ella said, pointing to a plate of lasagne. 'Do you want me to put it in the microwave for you?'

I'd already eaten three mouthfuls by the time she got to the end of her sentence. ''s fine like 'iss,' I said through a mouthful of cheese.

Lucy was putting away cutlery very slowly and

sadly. Amelia looked at me and Ella. None of us knew what to say.

'You okay, Luce?' I asked.

Lucy sighed. 'I miss Mrs Partridge. Normally, after tea I like to tell her how delicious my food was and how gross hers was.'

'That's ... really ... something,' Amelia said.

'You two were good friends,' Ella said. 'I bet she was glad that she came to live next door to you.'

Lucy thought about it. 'Yes, she was lucky. I wish she didn't die but it must have been nice for her to be my friend.'

Lucy actually looked happier already.

'Let me get this straight,' Amelia said. 'You're coming to terms with Mrs Partridge's death because even though it's sad that she's gone we can all hold on to the happy thought that at least when she was alive, her life had meaning and pleasure because she managed to meet you.'

Lucy nodded solemnly.

Amelia attempted not to explode with laughter, but a little bit bubbled out around the edges.

'I think Lucy means she's concentrating on what a long and happy life Mrs Partridge had,' Ella said.

'By meeting me,' Lucy added.

Amelia dissolved into giggles.

'You two did have a good time together,' I said

quickly, so that Lucy wouldn't start shouting at Amelia. 'I'm glad you feel better about it.'

'I still miss her. Mum says that's part of caring about someone and remembering them.'

Amelia stopped sniggering.

Lucy looked down at the floor. 'But it still hurts.'

She suddenly looked very small and very miserable.

Amelia knelt down and wrapped Lucy in a hug.

'I don't like it!' she wailed. I looked at Ella and we joined in the hug.

Lucy cried and cried and told us that it felt horrible and that she didn't understand it. When she'd finished, Amelia went and got her duvet and tucked her up on the sofa. She made us all hot chocolate and we watched a film. After that Lucy wasn't so angry, just quietly sad. Mum said that would get better but when you lose someone a bit of sadness always stays with you.

CHAPTER ✽ THIRTY–THREE

When we arrived at Dad's house on Wednesday afternoon, Suvi handed Amelia a large envelope.

'I sent away for this,' Suvi said. 'I thought you might be interested.'

Amelia managed to squeeze a tight little 'Thanks' out of the corner of her mouth.

Suvi looked at Ella and me. 'Kirsti is watching Lucy make fruit salad. Do you want to help?'

Ella and I went into the kitchen but Amelia crammed her envelope into her school bag and went upstairs.

I chopped up the apples and pears that Suvi gave me. I glanced across at Ella. I knew it was her assembly the next day, but she laughed hard when Kirsti patted my front with a banana-covered hand so I hoped she wasn't too stressed out by it.

When I went upstairs to change out of my banana-y shirt I found Amelia sitting on her bed, staring at something in her lap.

'What's that?' I asked.

'A prospectus.'

'What's a prospectus?'

'It's like a brochure for a school.'

'What have you got that for? You already go to school.'

'It's a performing arts school.'

'What, like drama school? You can't go to one of those till you're eighteen, can you?'

'This one starts in Year Seven.'

I had no idea that there were special schools that started so young. 'No way! Do they just do drama all day? Are there any special sports schools? I want to go to one.'

Amelia shook her head. 'You don't just do drama all day. Or sports. You still have to do GCSEs and everything.'

'Oh.' I was less interested now.

'But you focus on performing arts. So you can take dance, drama, and music GCSE.'

'And no maths?'

'Still maths. I think you have to take maths at every school.'

'What's the point, then? You can take dance and drama and music at our school.'

'No, you can't. You're only allowed to choose one of those for GCSE. And that's not the only thing; this whole school is set up to make you a great performer. They put on loads of concerts and shows and they have special tutors come in.' Her eyes were all shiny. 'Just imagine how brilliant it would be to be constantly working on your technique.'

I felt tired just thinking about it. 'Haven't you already chosen your GCSEs?'

Amelia's face fell. 'Yeah. I think it's probably too late for me to apply for September.'

'Why are you looking at it then?'

Amelia hesitated. 'Suvi gave it to me. This is what she sent off for.' She looked at me expectantly.

'I don't know why you're surprised,' I said. 'I know you don't like her, but actually Suvi is always doing nice things for people round here.'

Amelia's cheeks were flushed. 'I never said I didn't like her. I just . . . I'm surprised that she got this for me because I thought she thought I was rubbish at singing.'

'Why would you think that?'

'Because she's never said I'm good.'

I tried to remember a time when Suvi had

complimented Amelia's singing. I couldn't think of one and yet I was certain that Suvi *did* think Amelia was talented. 'She's not a very saying-things sort of person,' I tried to explain. 'She asked you to sing for her sister when she came to visit at Christmas, didn't she?'

'Yeah, but I thought she was just being polite.'

'Suvi's not a being-polite sort of person either. She says what she thinks.'

'Like Gabrielle's a better singer than me.'

'She didn't say that. She said that in show business people get chosen for their looks. That's true. Some of those men in boy bands can't sing at all.'

Amelia was obviously thinking. 'I still can't believe she did this.'

'It's because she's a doing-things sort of person.'

Amelia nodded slowly. 'I think you're right. And she wouldn't have sent for this if she didn't think I was good enough to go to a school like this.'

'Exactly!'

'Wow.' She stood up. 'I think I need to have a chat with Suvi.' And she went downstairs. I was so happy to think that Amelia was finally getting the idea that Suvi is really nice that I did a flying roly-poly on her bed.

Because I'm a doing-things sort of person too.

CHAPTER ❧ THIRTY–FOUR

It's strange being a sister. When you care about your sisters, you end up caring about all sorts of silly stuff that you never thought mattered, because it's a big deal to your sister. So that's why, on Thursday morning, I was sitting on the edge of my chair, feeling way more interested in an assembly than I have ever been in my life, apart from the time those people from the chocolate company came in and gave out free samples.

I don't normally get nervous about things, but watching Ella on the stage getting paler and paler, my stomach twisted itself into a knot and my mouth went paper-dry. Was this what Ella felt like all the time? I wasn't wrong when I said that she's tougher than you think. If I felt that way, I would want to stay at home under a duvet; I would not be carrying on doing the thing that made me feel like that.

First, we had to listen to one of the prefects introducing this student mentor thing that they want to do. Basically they want people from Year Nine upwards to volunteer to be mentors to people who are having problems in school. The idea is that the mentor is someone to talk to and someone to help you make plans to sort stuff out. Then the prefect sat down and Ella stood up. I could see her legs were shaking.

There was a pause.

She swallowed.

I decided that if she completely froze, I would just get up and blow a really loud raspberry to take the attention away from her.

But then she opened her mouth. I couldn't hear the first thing she said, she was too quiet.

'... really exciting opportunity for us to help each other and to improve our school.'

That was better. She was warming up.

She went on to tell us about a school in London where they had put in this sort of mentoring system and how the percentage of students who rated themselves as happy and confident at school had shot up. She also said that the research available on mentoring showed it could improve attendance rates and even GCSE results. It actually sounded like quite a good idea.

Ella looked up from her notes. 'In conclusion, I'd like to encourage anyone who is interested to sign up to be a mentor. By helping each other we can help our school move forward.'

That was it. She'd done it. People were clapping. I clapped too. And stamped my feet.

I was so pleased for her. Not only had she actually managed to stand up there and get through it, but I had heard almost every single word. I looked at Ella. Her pale face was starting to flush pink. She lifted her head and I gave her a big smile. She made a show of letting her shoulders drop. She looked about as relieved as a person who has just managed to avoid being eaten by a particularly terrifying monster. I was nearly bursting with how proud I was of Ella. I tried to show her by giving her a really enthusiastic thumbs-up. I ended up sticking my right thumb up Thunder's nose, which isn't a place anyone really wants to go, but I think Ella got the idea.

After all that it was a bit of a let-down to have to go to history but I spent the time making a plan. At lunchtime I found Amelia in the canteen.

'Wasn't Ella brilliant?' I asked her.

'She did really well, didn't she? I bet she's glad it's over.'

'Uh-huh. I was thinking we should have a Whoopee for her.'

In my family when one of us does something good like getting a swimming certificate or passing a ballet exam we have a sort of party called a Whoopee.

'Oh!' Amelia said. 'That's a good idea. What about Lucy, though? I don't think she's exactly in the mood for a Whoopee.'

I hadn't thought of that. 'But Ella has done something that was really hard for her and she did it brilliantly. That definitely deserves a Whoopee.'

'I'm not saying we shouldn't congratulate Ella, I just don't want to upset Lucy.'

I didn't want to give up on the idea. 'How about a tiny Whoopee?'

'How do we make a Whoopee tiny?'

I wasn't sure of the answer to that, but I'm not the kind of person who has to sort out every little detail before they go ahead with a plan so I just said, 'Leave it to me.'

Amelia asked Ella to go to the shops with her on the way home from school so that I could get things ready. First, I made my super-easy brownies and got them into the oven, then I went upstairs to decorate. Normally, when we have a Whoopee, we decorate the person we're celebrating's whole bedroom, but since we were going small scale I decided to just decorate a bit of Ella and Lucy's room. First, I got a sheet and tucked the long edge under Lucy's top bunk mattress so that it hung down, curtaining off Ella's bed. We used to do the same thing to make a base when we were little. I thought it would help to make the Whoopee small and private. I'd made some tiny paper chains during French (it was a nice change to do something useful in French for once). I strung them on the underside of Lucy's bunk so they were dangling over Ella's bed.

Back in the kitchen, the brownies were still cooking so I made a pile of weeny sandwiches. I looked for the smallest drinks I could find; in the end I decided on those yogurty things in little bottles that Mum drinks. The brownies were done so I put them out to cool, then cut them into tiny cubes and put everything on a tray. Now I had a miniature feast for our tiny Whoopee. I took everything to Ella's bedroom and that's when I heard someone on the stairs.

'Clo, are you ready?' Amelia called.

'Yep, come on up!'

Ella walked in. 'What's all this?' she asked looking at the sheet. 'Are we playing a game?'

'Look inside!' I said.

She pulled open the sheet curtain.

'Whoopee!' I whispered.

'Oh, Chloe! Is this for me?'

'Of course it's for you,' Amelia said. 'You were brilliant today.' She dropped her voice to a whisper too. 'Whoopee!'

'Thank you. Why are we whispering?'

'It's a tiny Whoopee,' I explained. 'We didn't want to upset Lucy.'

'Doesn't she want to come?'

I looked at Amelia. 'Actually we didn't ask.'

Right on cue we heard the door open and Mum called, 'We're back!' and Lucy added, 'From stupid school, but now there's only one day left till half-term!'

'I'll ask her,' Ella said. 'Whoopees are for the whole family.'

All three of us ran downstairs to speak to Lucy and Mum.

'How was your speech?' Mum asked.

'Okay,' Ella said.

'She was excellent,' I said, hugging Ella. 'Really clear and loud. We're about to have a Whoopee for her.'

'That's a lovely idea,' Mum said, though her eyes flicked to Lucy.

'It's just a small one,' I said. 'We didn't know if you'd feel like it, Lucy.'

'Do you?' Ella asked her.

Lucy pulled a bug-eyed face at us. 'Of course I'm coming to the Whoopee. It's not a Whoopee unless I'm there.'

So it ended up with all five of us trying to squish on to Ella's bed. Lucy insisted that I sat on her lap and then rolled about complaining I was breaking her legs. Mum added little cheesy biscuits and a big bag of M and M's to our tiny feast and we played music and did bed-dancing and talked about Ella's assembly.

It was a tiny Whoopee, but it was huge fun.

CHAPTER ✤ THIRTY-FIVE

I woke up on Saturday morning with that brilliant first-day-of-half-term feeling. It's so good having a week stretching in front of you to do whatever you like without any boring school getting in the way.

Except, I didn't exactly have lot of plans. There was no rugby training, no rugby camp and now not even Adrenaline Club. I started to feel a lot less brilliant. Then I remembered what Amirah had said about going back to rugby. I hated the idea of admitting I was wrong. I'd been so angry with Coach and I'd honestly thought he was being completely unfair. But now ... now I could see that being good at something isn't enough. If you want to succeed you've got to really care about it and not give up when things get tough, like Ella with her speech. You've got to keep on when you're disappointed, like Amelia after she didn't get the Amy part. And even if you're a crazy fun-loving person, sometimes you have to take things seriously, like Lucy with her determination to make money. Rushing around a rugby pitch is brilliant fun, but if I was going to do really well at it, I had to do the stuff I wasn't so keen on, like all the exercises and cleaning my boots.

And apologising to my coach.

I knew what I had to do so I got out of bed and got dressed ready to do it.

When I got down to Langley Fields, Coach was laying out cones while the squad were running laps. He raised his eyebrows when he saw me.

'Hi,' I said.

'Chloe, it's grand to see you.'

'I want to say sorry,' I blurted out. Then I hesitated; I hadn't really thought through my big apology any more than that.

'Oh aye?'

'I'm sorry that I got all upset about not being chosen for camp and I'm sorry that I quit the squad and I'm sorry that I skipped sessions and that I wasn't really, you know, giving it everything I've got.'

'You're a brave lass to get that out. Apology accepted.' He looked thoughtful. 'I hope I'm not so very strict with you girls; I want you to have your fun.'

'It is fun! I love it. I've missed it so much. There's some hard work with the fun but I don't mind that, honest.'

He smiled.

'So can I come back? Please? I promise I'll be on my best behaviour and I'll never whinge about anything and you can play me in any position and I'll help with all the equipment an—'

'Steady on! Don't be trying to turn into a saint all in one. Of course you can come back. We'll be glad to have you.'

And then, even though Coach is not exactly the cuddly type, I couldn't help hugging him, and the girls must have seen us and worked out what it meant because I heard someone shout, 'Chloe's coming back!' and there was a big cheer. Coach fought me off and ruffled my hair and I felt super happy because it's nice to know that even though I'd made some mistakes; people still like me.

Because it was the first day of half-term, Mum took us to Pizza Hut for tea. Amelia talked about singing for the entire time it took me to eat my pizza. That's not as long as you might think because I can eat a pizza pretty fast, but she was still going when we got to ice cream.

'. . . and we got matinee tickets for *Little Women* so Lauren can still get to bed early.'

'Are you going to watch that?' Lucy asked. 'Isn't that the thing that they didn't want you for?'

There was a hush while we waited to see if Amelia could keep her temper with Lucy over that one.

'It's good to watch other performers,' Amelia said quite calmly. 'Besides, I'm over all that; Suvi says that in an uncertain career like singing you have to focus on what you can control and not get upset about what you can't.'

I had never heard Amelia say 'Suvi says' before and I don't think Mum had either because her eyelids did this weird little flicker before she said, 'That's good advice.'

'So . . . remember you said if I was good I could have singing lessons?' Amelia asked.

Mum wiped her mouth with a napkin. 'Mm hmm.'

'Have I been good?'

Mum thought about it. 'You have.'

I had to agree with that. 'You haven't tried to strangle any of us for ages.'

226

Amelia narrowed her eyes at me.

'What?' I said. 'I'm trying to help you out here!'

Amelia ignored me. 'Also, because it's important that I take responsibility for my career . . .'

I wondered if that was something that Suvi had said as well.

'. . . I want to contribute towards the lessons, so I've got a job.'

'A job!' Mum's eyes bulged.

'You're not old enough for a job,' Lucy said.

'It's not a big job. And I'm fourteen, not a baby.'

'What are you going to do?' Ella asked.

'She won't be doing anything until I've approved it,' Mum said.

'Well . . .' said Amelia, flicking back her hair, and I knew we were in for a long story. 'What I wanted to do was work at the theatre. But they said I was too young to do anything. Not even the box office, which is silly because it's not like you even need to be good at maths; the till does all the adding up for you. And I did point out that if I worked backstage no one would be able to see me, so no one would know if I was a bit on the young side, but they didn't go for that. What they did say I could do was deliver their little booklets about upcoming performances. So . . . four times a year

I'm going to be a top-class booklet distributor and deliver five hundred of the things around town.'

'Wow,' Mum said. 'You've certainly been busy.'

'They said you had to ring them to say it was okay.' She fluttered her eyelashes at Mum. 'So, can I do it?'

'I should think so. Although, I'd prefer it if you took one of your friends or Chloe when you do your delivering and you mustn't be out after dark.'

Amelia nodded. 'I know I won't be earning all the time, but it will be enough to pay for some of my lessons.'

Mum smiled. 'Maybe we'll keep enough back for you to buy a little something nice for yourself as well.'

CHAPTER 🍓 THIRTY-SIX

Back at home I took my rugby ball out into the garden to practise, but Lucy followed me and stared over the fence into Mr Partridge's garden with a sad face.

'You have to do a thing for me,' she said.

'Do I?'

'Yes.'

'Why?'

'Because.'

Sometimes conversations are like this with Lucy. I looked her up and down. She was still looking pale and tired. 'All right,' I said. 'I'll do it. What is it?'

'I can't tell you all of it.'

I nearly said it was okay anyway, but then I remembered that chat with Dad about being a leader and not getting people into trouble. I mean, Lucy doesn't need any help from me to get into trouble but I knew I mustn't let her do anything stupid.

'Is it dangerous?' I asked.

'No.'

'Could anyone get hurt?'

'No.'

'Will Mum be cross?'

'No.'

'What do I have to do?'

'Just take me to a shop. It's not far. I'm not allowed to go by myself.'

'You're not going to try to buy fireworks, are you?'

'No.'

I couldn't think of any more questions so I promised I would take her once I'd done a bit of practice.

Lucy went back into the house with one last look over the fence. Ten minutes later Ella came out with a book and a blanket, but I persuaded her to help me practise my catching.

'Can I ask you something?' I said to her.

'Okay.'

'How do you do it?'

'Do what?'

'Be good. All the time. It's exhausting.'

Ella tilted her head on one side. 'I don't know. I don't exactly try.'

A squawky noise like a surprised parrot came out of me. 'You don't even try! How is that possible? It's like when I was born they didn't give me any good at all and they saved it all up for you.'

'Don't be silly. There are lots of good things in you. You're very kind; you're always doing things for your sisters and your friends.'

'But that isn't helping me be perfectly behaved all the time.'

'Did Mum and Dad say you have to be good all the time now, because of your dare club thing?'

'Not exactly. Dad said I had to be a good influence. And not encourage people to do naughty things. So I'm trying to be good around Thunder and save my bad thoughts for when I'm at home. I spent half an hour last night thinking about the best kind of pie to throw in Mr Chadwick's face.'

'What kind is it?'

'Mud and worm.' I slapped a hand over my mouth. 'I shouldn't have said that. I'm not going to do it. But I have to think of some bad things or I'll explode.'

'I think it's probably okay to think about pies in Mr Chadwick's face.'

'But you don't, do you?'

'Mr Chadwick is pretty mean. Even when I tell him the right answers to questions he tells me off for saying it too quietly. I might occasionally think about a pie in his face now that you've mentioned it.'

'Noooo! Don't do it because I said it. That's exactly what I'm not supposed to be doing.'

Ella patted my arm. 'All right. I won't. I'll go back to thinking about him having a music lesson with Mr Garcia.'

That made me laugh. The only teacher meaner than Mr Chadwick is Mr Garcia and I bet Mr Chadwick can't even play a triangle. I was surprised that Ella had been thinking about ways to torture Mr Chadwick. Was it okay for me to be thinking those sorts of things?

'You're worrying too much,' Ella said.

'Hold on, isn't that what I usually say to you?'

'I don't think Dad is expecting you to be an angel; I think he just wants you to be careful about how you influence people.'

I flopped down on the grass. 'Ugh. It's just boring. All this thinking hard about everything I do and trying to be a good example makes me feel not very Chloe-ish.'

Ella spread out her blanket and offered me a

spot. 'I still don't think you get it. He wants you to be the best leader that you can be. That means looking after other people and encouraging people to do their best.'

'Does it?'

'Yes! And you're brilliant at all those things.'

'Am I?'

'Yes, look at the way you've supported me through doing this speech. And what about the way you always manage to change the subject when Lucy and Amelia are about to get into a fight.'

Lucy banged on the kitchen window and I held up one finger to show her I would be there in a minute. I turned back to Ella.

'But I don't do those things to be a leader or anything; I just do that kind of stuff because it seems like a good thing to do.'

'That's exactly what I mean. Dad just wants you to keep throwing yourself into tough jobs in the strong, kind way that you already do. And that,' she smiled at me, 'is *completely* Chloe.'

I felt much better.

CHAPTER 🍓 THIRTY–SEVEN

Monday was Mrs Partridge's wake. I didn't know what a wake was, but Mum said it was like a party to celebrate the life of someone who had died.

'Mr Partridge asked if Lucy wanted to come,' she told me while I was helping her round up all the school uniform for washing.

'Is Lucy going to go?' I asked.

'Yes, I'm taking her. I hope it will be a good opportunity for her to say goodbye to Mrs Partridge.'

I had a sneaking suspicion that she was also hoping that Lucy wouldn't have a complete meltdown and start punching people because she was angry that Mrs Partridge had died.

'Do you want me to come too?' I asked. I thought that if Lucy did start having a tantrum I could just throw her over my shoulder and bring her home.

Mum looked up from the pile of grubby shirts she was cramming into the washing-machine. 'Oh, Chloe, Would you mind? I think it might be helpful if she had one of you girls to talk to. I imagine everyone else there will be quite old.'

I gave her a thumbs-up. 'Sure.'

'Thank you, sweetheart.' She clicked the washing-machine door shut. 'Although, I should just be really clear that when I said it was a party, I didn't mean the kind you're used to. Mostly it will be standing about talking in low voices and I'll need you to be quiet and respectful.'

That didn't sound like a party to me at all. 'Don't worry, Mum, I won't dance on any tables.'

We set off for the wake at ten past two and we arrived thirty seconds later. I pointed out that we could have cut that time right down if we'd climbed over the wall between our front garden and Mr Partridge's but Mum just whispered, 'Remember, quiet and respectful' at me through gritted teeth.

Mr Partridge opened the door and Mum launched into telling him how sorry she was about Mrs Partridge and what a lovely lady she was.

Lucy screwed up her face when she heard that and opened her mouth to tell us what Mrs Partridge was really like.

'I like your house!' I said quickly.

'Er, yes,' Mum said. 'And what gorgeous flowers.'

There was a huge basket of them at the foot of the stairs.

'Mm,' said Mr Partridge. 'House is full of them. I should have thought to say donations only. I can't think who's sent all the messy things. There's no name on most of them.'

We'd reached the sitting room by then and he wasn't kidding; there were brightly coloured flowers on every surface. Vases and jugs and baskets full of them on the table, the dresser, the coffee table and the windowsill. The reds and yellows and pinks of the petals really perked up the boring brown and cream room. I could see through to the kitchen where there were yet more bunches laid on the counter still in their cellophane wrappings. Lucy looked around at them with bright eyes and a wide smile.

I had a suspicion.

On Saturday, when Lucy had finally revealed that the shop she wanted me to take her to was the florist's, I was quite happy to walk her there and I even agreed to wait outside. I'd assumed that she was ordering the normal amount of flowers that you send when someone has died, i.e. one bunch, but looking at Lucy's delighted face now I was pretty sure that she had decided what to do with all the money she'd earned: she hadn't just spent it on something she liked; she'd spent it on something that both she and Mrs Partridge liked: flowers. Hundreds of flowers.

'They're beautiful,' I said. 'I think Mrs Partridge would have loved them.'

Lucy smiled the biggest smile that I'd seen on her face since Mrs Partridge had died.

Mr Partridge gestured round the room. 'I don't know what I'm going to do with them after the wake.'

'I could take them to Mrs Partridge's grave if you like,' Lucy said.

Mr Partridge hasn't got a very agreeing type of face. Before you've even said anything, his eyes are not interested, and his mouth is all drawn up ready to push out a short sharp 'no'. So when Lucy said that, it took a while for Mr Partridge's 'no' face to melt away, but it did go away and when it did, he looked younger and less cross. I think he was actually quite pleased that Lucy had offered.

Mum must have thought so too because she said, 'Yes, if you wanted, we could help Lucy do that for you. Your mother was very fond of flowers, wasn't she?'

'She liked tulips best,' Lucy said.

Mr Partridge nodded and I was surprised to see that his eyes were a bit watery.

It was sort of nice to know that even someone who is grumpy with little girls still loves their mum.

The wake was very boring. The only good things were the sausage rolls and that there were a couple of Mrs Partridge's ancient friends there who really enjoyed hearing Lucy talk about Mrs Partridge. Apart from that, it was just like Mum said: people standing round talking very quietly. My wake is going to be a proper celebration, with big pictures of me projected onto the walls and all my sporting trophies on display. There'll be music and singing and dancing.

When everyone had gone, Mum helped one of Mrs Partridge's nieces tidy up, while Lucy and I loaded all the flowers into Mum's car. Then Mum drove us to the cemetery. It took a while before all the flowers were arranged how Lucy wanted them. There were so many that they were spilling onto the graves on either side.

'That's okay,' Lucy said. 'Mrs Partridge says flowers are for sharing.'

Mum and I moved a little further away so that Lucy could have a last goodbye with Mrs Partridge.

'Please tell me that you went with her to the florist's,' Mum said in a low voice.

I turned to look at her; how on earth did she know about that? I hoped I wasn't in trouble.

'I did go with her but I thought she was just sending one lot. How did you know they were from Lucy?'

'I'm a mum, that's what I do. I pick up dirty socks and I know things.' She looked over at the stacked bunches of flowers. 'Also, people don't normally send tulips for a funeral.'

Now that I thought about it, Lucy's flowers were all very bright and bunchy; they looked nothing like the neat white arrangements in baskets and cross shapes that people sent for my nana's funeral.

'She certainly got a lot for her money, didn't she?' I said.

'I'm sure she was very charming with the lady in the flower shop.'

It was pretty impressive the way that Mum had worked out what Lucy had done and that she totally understood why Lucy had done it. It makes you feel better when people understand you. I'd been feeling pretty lousy for a while because it seemed like no one quite got how sorry I was about the whole Adrenaline Club thing. I looked up at Mum. 'Do you know things about me?'

She reached an arm around my shoulders and pulled me closer. 'I know that you are trying very hard to make up for mistakes you've made by being good.'

I felt a little skip inside. Maybe she did know how I felt. 'Really?'

'Really. I can tell. Although, I don't think you need to worry too much, because even though you sometimes do crazy things, you already were good. You've got a good, kind heart, Chloe.' She gave me a cuddle. I felt the last little bits of worry melt away. I'd done some silly things but everything was going to be all right.

'Do you know what?' I asked. 'I think I might be able to manage this being a brilliant natural leader after all.'

Mum laughed. 'I never had any doubts.'

Then I let go of Mum and put my arms out to Lucy because she'd finished saying goodbye and she needed her own cuddle.

CHAPTER ❤ THIRTY-EIGHT

At breakfast the next morning, Lucy seemed a lot like her usual self. I could tell because she snatched the Coco Pops box out of my hand and said, 'If you've eaten all of them, I will mash your head like a potato.'

It was nice to hear her sounding so cheerful.

Amelia was still in bed and Mum was on her laptop in the sitting room, but Ella looked up from her book. 'I can go to the corner shop and get some more Coco Pops if we need them.'

I shook my head. 'There's enough left for Lucy and I haven't got time for seconds. I'm going to help Coach with the under-tens' Rugby Fun Day.'

'Do you not want to go?' Lucy asked. 'Because you look like you're about to swallow something disgusting.'

I realised I was pulling a bit of a face so I tried to rearrange my mouth into a smile.

'Nana used to say that if you've got to swallow a frog then you might as well do it cheerfully,' Ella said, buttering a piece of toast.

'It's amazing the way you can remember all the stuff that Nana used to come out with,' I said. Nana talked a lot of nonsense, but I suppose that the Fun Day was a bit like swallowing a frog. I didn't really want to do it. I volunteered because Coach needed help and I thought it would be an excellent way of setting a good example. Still, Nana was right; there was no point in doing a good thing if I was going to be grumpy about it.

'I'm sure it'll be great,' I said. 'I'm going to show these titchers all my best moves.'

'I hope you have a good time,' Ella said.

'I hope you trip over your big feet and land in the mud,' Lucy said.

The fun day was at Langley Fields. When I arrived, there was a mob of little kids surrounding Coach. They were mostly boys but I was pleased to see two girls standing together on the edge of the crowd.

'Right,' Coach said, clapping his hands. 'Let's get started. First off, we're going to play a wee warm-up game called Kicking Donkey. My assistant here –' he pointed at me – 'is going to show you what to do.'

'She can't play rugby,' one of the little squirts said. 'She's a girl.'

What an idiot. Here I was trying to be helpful and some brat was coming out with this nonsense.

'Can she not?' Coach said in an icy voice. 'Well, let's have a look-see, shall we?' He turned to me. 'Chloe, demonstrate to this young man how you can't kick a ball.'

I was so angry that what I really wanted to do was bash the kid, but then I saw the two girls watching hard; they were here to see rugby, not wrestling. So I set the ball on the ground, took a run up and ... sent the ball sailing over the crossbar.

The kids all gasped like a firework had just gone off. It was great. The little squirt didn't say anything more about girls and rugby after that.

I'd thought the day would drag, but by the time we'd done some warm-up games and talked them through the basics of the rules, it was time for a break and a drink. After that, we worked on drills; Coach had me demonstrate and then I got to work my way round the groups helping them out. The kids were mostly pretty rubbish to start with, but it was actually quite satisfying to watch them get the hang of it. When the two girls did a perfect switch pass I found myself punching the air. Coaching is fun.

After lunch, we played a mini match and the kids all tried so hard; I was really pleased with them. When their parents started arriving to pick them up I was kind of sad the whole thing was finished.

'Are you doing any more Fun Days?' I asked Coach.

'Not this half-term but there'll be several in the summer holidays.'

'Brilliant. I mean, can I help again? At all of them? Can I see if my little sister wants to come?'

Coach smiled. 'Aye, you can do that.' He gave me that studying look he does. 'Of course, you never know, if you work really hard, you might not be able to make it to all of the Fun Days.' He patted me on the shoulder. 'You might be away at a training camp.'

I did a double-take. Did he mean what I thought he meant? 'Really? You might choose me for a camp?'

'If you put the time and effort in.'

I was so happy that I did three cartwheels followed by a round-off.

And I was in such a good mood that when Little Squirt asked me to show him how to do it, I did.

Can't get enough of the
STRAWBERRY SISTERS?

Want to know how to set up your
own Adrenaline Club? Or what
your STRAWBERRY SISTER
hobby is?

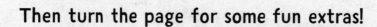

Then turn the page for some fun extras!

STRAWBERRY SISTERS PROFILES

AMELIA
Age: 14

🍓 Hobbies: singing about sad things, painting her nails black and being sarcastic

🍓 Favourite food: pizza

🍓 Favourite phrase: **'That's a stupid idea'**

🍓 Dream job: singer in a band

CHLOE
Age: 12

🍓 Hobbies: wrestling, hockey, rugby (if you can knock your teeth out doing it, Chloe loves it)

🍓 Favourite food: curry, chocolate and cake (sometimes all at the same time)

🍓 Favourite phrase: **'Can I have some more?'**

🍓 Dream job: crisp taster

ELLA
Age: 11

🍓 Hobbies: making films with Ashandra and karaoke with Kayleigh

🍓 Favourite food: brownies

🍓 Favourite phrase: 'I'll do it'

🍓 Dream job: working with numbers and nice people

LUCY
Age: 7

🍓 Hobbies: ballet, magic and being a bat

🍓 Favourite food: spaghetti with tomato ketchup

🍓 Favourite phrase: 'NO!'

🍓 Dream job: magician or Bat Queen

KIRSTI
Age: 0

🍓 Hobbies: dribbling, sleeping and gurgling

🍓 Favourite food: milk

🍓 Favourite phrase: 'Waaaaaaaaah!'

🍓 Dream job: cot tester

STRAWBERRY SISTERS QUIZ: WHAT'S YOUR STRAWBERRY SISTER HOBBY?

WHAT IS YOUR FAVOURITE WAY TO RELAX?
a) Reading a book.
b) Shutting myself in my room and singing really loudly.
c) Running around to burn off lots of energy.
d) Coming up with lots of new insults.

YOUR BEST FRIEND IS MISERABLE. HOW DO YOU CHEER HER UP?
a) Take her for a milkshake and be extra nice to her.
b) Decorate her room for her as a nice surprise.
c) Think up a really good dare for her to do.
d) Tease her and tell her lots of jokes.

WHAT'S YOUR IDEAL WAY OF SPENDING A WEEKEND?
a) Finishing my homework and hanging out with my friends.
b) Going shopping, talking about cute boys, singing in my choir.
c) Playing sports and eating all my favourite foods.
d) Finding someone to shout my new insults at.

IF YOU COULD HAVE ANY PET, WHAT WOULD YOU CHOOSE?
a) A rabbit.
b) A cat.
c) A dog that can do tricks.
d) A bat, or something with really sharp teeth.

WHAT WOULD YOU SAY IS YOUR BEST QUALITY?
a) I'm nice and friendly.
b) I'm a brilliant singer.
c) I'm fast and strong.
d) Everything about me is brilliant.

HOW WOULD YOUR FRIENDS DESCRIBE YOU?
a) Hardworking and loyal.
b) A star in the making.
c) Daring and fun.
d) The best.

IT'S OWN CLOTHES DAY AT SCHOOL. WHAT DO YOU WEAR?
a) My jeans and a nice top.
b) Something that coordinates with what my best friend is
   wearing.
c) My comfiest shorts and t-shirt.
d) My new tutu.

WHAT KIND OF FILMS DO YOU LIKE BEST?
a) Something romantic and happy.
b) Something that makes me cry.
c) Something full of action and explosions.
d) Something with talking animals.

WHAT'S YOUR BEST SUBJECT AT SCHOOL?
a) Maths.
b) Music.
c) PE.
d) Making the teacher cry.

WHAT WOULD BE YOUR IDEAL JOB?
a) Something quiet, that doesn't involve public speaking – maybe in a library.
b) A professional singer.
c) Something outdoorsy and sporty – maybe a rugby coach!
d) Anything that involves making lots of money!

TURN THE PAGE FOR THE ANSWERS . . .

MOSTLY 'A'S

You're like Ella. You're quiet and hardworking and very loyal to your friends. You don't like being the centre of attention so your favourite hobby would be something you can do on your own, like reading, drawing, or writing stories.

MOSTLY 'B'S

You're like Amelia. Your friends think you're wonderful and you love being the star of the show! Your favourite hobby would be something like singing or acting, anything where you can take centre-stage.

MOSTLY 'C'S

You're like Chloe. You love sport, running around, all sorts of food, and anything that gets your adrenaline going! Your favourite hobby would be something like rugby, football or netball.

MOSTLY 'D'S

You're like Lucy. You're loud and full of mischief and always on the look-out for fun. Your favourite hobby might be something like taking lots of annoying photographs of your friends and family in silly situations.

THUNDER'S RECIPE FOR EASY CHOCOLATE BROWNIES

INGREDIENTS
400G JAR OF CHOCOLATE SPREAD
60G SELF-RAISING FLOUR
2 EGGS

YOU'LL ALSO NEED A PAN AND SOME
BAKING PAPER

METHOD
Ask a grown-up to pre-heat the oven to 180 C / Gas 4. Line a
20x30cm pan with baking paper. Plop everything in a bowl and
stir until it's all mixed up. (If you 'clean' the jar by scraping it
out with your fingers, don't do what Thunder did and get your
hand stuck in the jar!)

Pour the mixture into the pan and bake for about 25 minutes
until the top looks light brown and speckly, like Amelia's nose
when she's been out in the sun for too long.

Let them cool for as long as you can bear to wait, then cut into
squares and eat until your mum says you're not allowed any more!

CHLOE'S GUIDE TO ADRENALINE CLUB

1. Gather together a group of your bravest friends. Great, now you have your very own Adrenaline Club!

2. Adrenaline Club is a secret society – so no one outside of the club is allowed to know it exists.

3. Take it in turns to each think up a really daring dare that will give you an adrenaline rush. Write them down as a list. But don't forget – it's important to make sure none of the dares are dangerous or against any rules.

4. It's called Adrenaline Club, not Everybody-Have-A-Nice-Relaxing-Day Club, so when one person does a dare, make sure you give them a big high-five!

5. When everyone in Adrenaline Club has completed the same dare, tick it off your list and go on to the next one!

6. Never force anyone to do anything they don't want to. Just because you think of a dare, doesn't mean you have to do it.

"A TOUCHING STORY ABOUT SISTERS AND FRIENDSHIPS. GENTLE AND WARM AND FUNNY" – JACQUELINE WILSON

PERFECTLY ELLA

CANDY HARPER

"A TOUCHING STORY ABOUT SISTERS AND FRIENDSHIPS.
GENTLE AND WARM AND FUNNY"
JACQUELINE WILSON ON PERFECTLY ELLA

ESPECIALLY
AMELIA

CANDY
HARPER

Just like Ella, Candy Harper grew up in a rather small house with a rather large family. As the fourth of five sisters it was often hard to get a word in edgeways, so she started writing down her best ideas. It's probably not a coincidence that her first 'book' featured an orphan living in a deserted castle.

Growing up, she attended six different schools, but that honestly had very little to do with an early interest in explosives.

Candy has been a bookseller, a teacher and the person who puts those little stickers on apples. She is married and has a daughter named after Philip Pullman's Lyra.

You can follow her on Twitter @CandyHarper_